Melt
for Him

a Fighting Fire novel

Lauren Blakely

Entangled Publishing, LLC
2614 South Timberline Road
Suite 109
Fort Collins, CO 80525
Visit our website at www.entangledpublishing.com.

Brazen is an imprint of Entangled Publishing, LLC. For more information on our titles, visit www.brazenbooks.com.

Edited by Stacy Abrams andAlycia Tornetta
Cover design by Heather Howland
Cover art by Shutterstock

Manufactured in the United States of America

First Edition September 2014

This book is dedicated to all the brave men and women in the fire service.

Chapter One

She had killer legs.

Strong, shapely—the kind that should never be covered up with pants or jeans. Yeah, the woman who'd just walked into the alley behind his bar, as if she were hunting for a bit of peace and quiet, too, should be legally required to wear short skirts and boots every single day.

He'd happily sign that edict.

She headed in his direction, tapping away on her phone, and Becker saw no reason not to check her out from his post at a table on the back porch of the Panting Dog, the microbrewery he owned and operated. Considering the way the crowds inside had felt constricting, wanting to toast him and his good buddy Travis for simply doing their job—as volunteer firemen, they'd answered the call and saved two kids from a fast-moving midnight fire a few weeks ago—he'd had to get away for a bit. The quiet porch had much more appeal than the scene inside, which threatened to bring other memories careening back, too—memories with different endings. But here in the dark of the warm May night that surrounded him, he was trained on the present, only the present—and on those legs.

He raked his eyes over the rest of the woman.

The gorgeous brunette looked like she put a premium on fitness—maybe woke up early for hikes or a five-mile run as the sun rose, just as he did. She was toned all over, and he offered a silent thanks to the genius who invented strappy little tanks, because they'd clearly been designed with this woman in mind. On her wrist she had a gray leather band, like a bracelet, and that, coupled with a small tattoo on her shoulder, seemed to scream "tough chick." As she neared him, she stopped texting, tucked her phone into her purse, and tugged at the neckline of her shirt.

"Fuck it," she said and looked to the left, then to the right. She hadn't seen him. She reached a hand up the back of her shirt, and seconds later she'd unhooked a lacy white bra and was stuffing it into her purse alongside the phone.

The knowledge that her breasts were riding bareback against the tight tank made him instantly hard. The shadows were his friends, though, and the dark corner he'd set up camp in was far enough away from the nearby streetlamps, or she might have seen his jaw drop. She was an even greater sight to behold now, and he could barely take his eyes off the way the fabric hugged her breasts. A triple threat from the legs, to the breasts, to the face. He hoped to God she had all the other assets he liked, too, namely the ones upstairs.

He cycled through opening lines that wouldn't earn a roll of the eyes. But he didn't need lines, because she was making a beeline for the table, eyeing the chair across from him.

Maybe fate was in his favor tonight. Maybe she was what he needed to take his mind away from the noise and the chatter—both from inside his bar and from those damn memories that taunted him of all that had gone wrong in Chicago and sent him far away from the Windy City to set up a new home here in Hidden Oaks, California, deep in the heart of wine country. New life, new department, new friends. A new chance.

She wobbled.

She was a few feet away from the table, and she must have caught a rock or a pebble, because she lunged unevenly, starting to reach for the back of a chair. Reflexes kicking in, he rose quickly and steadied her with a sure hand on her elbow. She looked straight at him. There was the slightest touch of embarrassment in her face, but then it was quickly replaced by an amused determination.

She gave a quick wave, then smoothed over her skirt. "Nice to meet you. I'm Megan. I'm kind of a klutz sometimes," she said, owning it. She was both utterly adorable and unbelievably hot with the way she turned her stumble into a confident introduction.

"I'm Becker. I happen to be a big fan of klutzes."

She gave him an appreciative nod, as if to say, *Well played.* He pulled out the chair for her, and she sat down, crossing the bare legs that he longed to touch. If she went commando on top, did she downstairs as well?

A man could dream. A man could hope. A man could thank the lucky stars a claustrophobic evening had just turned into a night of possibility. He sat down quickly, because it was already getting tighter inside his jeans.

• • •

Hidden Oaks was just as Megan remembered when she left more than a year ago. All the shops were the same, that statue of the guy on a horse in the town square was the same, even the window displays at the olive oil specialty shop were the same. The only thing different was the bar where she'd planned to meet her friend Jamie before she'd taken the detour to the alley. The Panting Dog wasn't here a year ago, nor was this man.

She'd have noticed him. She'd have remembered him.

He wasn't exactly forgettable, even with the shadows across his face.

"I'm actually forbidden by the Klutz Association from wearing these boots," she said, picking up the thread of their banter and holding her leg out to show him the heel on her short red boots. "But I defied their orders."

"I won't tell them you're a scofflaw then," he said, in that warm and gravelly voice, the kind that could sell you whiskey or bourbon, or maybe even himself. Smooth but with a touch of something else—danger, perhaps. One faint streetlight shone across half his face, and the half she could see was hauntingly beautiful. Strong cheekbones, a touch of stubble, and dark eyes that looked as if they'd seen many things. Her eyes roamed to his arms, which seemed to be in a permanent state of flex. She bet he could lift a dresser and carry it easily, lay it in the bed of a truck with barely an effort. Because, yes, of course this man drove a truck. Probably red and scratched-up, the kind he'd drive to the end of a long dirt road with her, toss a blanket in the back, and then they'd get it on under the stars.

Hold on. They'd barely even exchanged words and she was already picturing tangoing with him in the back of a truck? That's what a good pair of arms did to her. Made her mind tumble ten steps ahead. She'd always loved a well-built man. So sue her for staring.

But she needed to focus on why she'd taken this detour for the alley in the first place—to be alone. There was a reason she hadn't stepped foot in the Panting Dog to hang out with Jamie, who managed the bar. When she'd peered through the window a few minutes ago, she had been met with the sight of a packed bar, patrons standing shoulder to shoulder, wedged inside. And after she'd spent most of her time in Los Angeles the last year trying to keep her ex away from that kind of scene, which had offered too many temptations to him, it was one of her least favorite sights. So she'd headed for the quiet of the back porch, hoping to read a book as she waited for Jamie to finish her shift.

But screw reading. As long as Becker wasn't a fireman or a drunk, she'd be keen on chatting for a few minutes. Not that she lumped drunks with firemen. Not at all. But either type was a deal-breaker, though for different reasons. The bottom line was the same—they both could pulverize a heart.

"Anything else the Klutzes forbid you from wearing?" he asked in a teasing tone, continuing the thread of their shared joke.

Oh. Had he seen her starting to strip? Seemed a strong possibility. And so why the hell not run with it?

"Why would you ask?" she said, running a finger along the strap of her tank top, as if she simply had to adjust it right this second.

"No reason at all," he said, trying to rein in a grin that threatened to curve up his lips. He tipped his forehead to Megan's shoulder. "I completely didn't notice that you were removing an article of clothing because I was trying to admire the ink on your skin. What's your tattoo there?"

She laughed loudly. "Nicely done," she said, her way of acknowledging that he hadn't quite taken the easy road by asking directly about the lingerie she'd already ditched. That damn strapless bra had been bugging her. And he'd clearly seen her take it off. But then, he'd already seen her stumble, so on the scope of things in life she should care about, the prospect of a stranger having seen her go through the first level of solo strip poker didn't bother her. Nor did it bug her that he was checking out the way her nipples were outlined against the cotton of her tank. Especially because she didn't really want him to be a stranger right then.

"The thing you didn't notice? I'm going to tell you a secret," she said playfully, owning her moment of nearly eating the sidewalk, and owning her lack of a seat belt for her breasts. "Strapless bras suck."

"I'm going to tell you a secret. You not wearing a bra right now? That doesn't suck."

She laughed, then patted her shoulder. "And to answer your question: that's my owl."

He leaned forward, the glow of the streetlamp illuminating him fully now, and *holy smokes*. He wasn't just gorgeous. He was the very definition of smoldering. His eyes were the deepest of browns, his cheekbones were chiseled, and his hair was dark with the slightest wave. But those eyes—somehow they said he was more than just a fine specimen of muscle, and height, and beauty. There was something hidden, something dark in the past, and that lured her in like a magnet. Because it was familiar.

"An owl? Let me guess. Does it have to do with being wise?" But before she could answer, he shook his head and spoke again. "No. I don't think it does. I bet there's some deeper meaning."

She tapped her finger to her nose. "Bingo."

"I could ask what it is, but I have a feeling you don't ink and tell."

"You're right. I don't always," she said. She hadn't even told her brother Travis, and they'd nearly raised each other at times. He didn't like that she'd gotten a tattoo. He was overprotective in every way, down to warning her not to ink her own body because he didn't trust tattoo shops. That was par for the course with Travis; he was skeptical and suspicious by nature, but then, those traits had served them both well when they were growing up.

But she could toss Becker a bone. He'd earned that much with his directness, not to mention his fast reflexes. "I'll tell you something else about my tattoo, though. I designed it myself," Megan added.

"So are you a tattoo artist?"

She shook her head wistfully. "Not yet, but I will be soon. I've been learning the trade, working with some artists, and I have a gig lined up that I'm super excited about. I've always loved to draw, though, and have been lucky enough to work as a freelance artist," she said. She'd been a freelance makeup artist in Los Angeles, and a freelance photographer, and a freelance illustrator. She was back in town on a freelance basis, too, since her brother had convinced her to hang out for a few weeks in Hidden Oaks to shoot the firemen's calendar. The regular photographer had left town to tend to some family matters, and the firehouse was in a pinch to produce the calendar quickly. It was a best seller, and all the proceeds benefited the local hospital's burn center, so Megan had agreed to donate her time and work for the cause.

The timing proved fortuitous. She wasn't going to stay long—she had Portland on her travel itinerary next, since she'd found out earlier that week that she'd landed an apprenticeship at one of the city's premier tattoo shops, where she'd be turning her designs into body art starting in June.

Hidden Oaks was a way station, then she'd head north. But she didn't want to go into all the details of her job history or job future with Becker. The night she met her ex, she'd been patently open with him, sharing details of her life, and look where that had gotten her—straight into a damaging relationship she'd only recently been able to untangle herself from. She would try a different tactic with this man. She would hold herself back. Protect her secrets and herself. She was no longer an open book.

"Well, Ms. Soon-to-Be Tattoo Artist, I don't believe we've had a proper handshake," he said, giving her a small smile. His large hand wrapped around Megan's, and she liked the way his skin felt against hers. She started wondering whether she'd like more skin-on-skin contact, and as she grew warmer between her thighs, she had her answer. *Yes.* She wanted to be closer to him. She leaned in, enjoying the heat that radiated from his body, too.

Maybe it was all physical. Or maybe it was more. Maybe it was because she didn't know him, and he didn't know her, and they could be anybody. They could be people without pasts, without stories, without baggage. A man, a woman, meeting by chance. A quick stumble, a brief catch, as if some-one or something had wanted them to meet. The night was a blank slate full of possibility. She started picturing those warm, strong hands on her, on her hips, on her waist, touch-ing her shoulders, and she shivered at the images flashing by.

"You're new to town, aren't you?" she asked.

"Moved here a year ago from Chicago. And you? You new, too?"

"I'm just passing through. Making my way up the coast," she said, and she liked the feel of that answer, how it suited the mood she'd been in lately—a mood for change, for new beginnings.

"Ah, you've got wanderlust."

"A traveling heart," she said.

"I'm glad you traveled into this alley tonight."

"Why are you hanging out in the dark by yourself?"

"I could ask you the same."

"Truth?"

"Sure. Might as well start there."

"I don't like parties," she admitted.

"I don't like crowds."

"Ah, so we have that in common."

"And that's why we find ourselves here in an alley."

"Besides hanging out solo in alleys on a Friday night, what is it that you do, Mr. Becker?" She was surprised at how incredibly flirtatious she sounded when she said his name, almost like Marilyn breathily whispering, "Mr. Presi-dent." But then Becker was the opposite of what she'd been used to for the last year. He seemed both straightforward and completely lacking in pretenses, and there was little more appealing to Megan than that. Well, except perhaps for his body, all carved and broad, and his eyes, so dark and penetrating. She imagined being underneath him, looking into their depths, feeling the intensity of his stare as he moved in her, the kind of gaze that could blot out all the bad memories.

He tipped his head to the back entrance of the Panting Dog. "I own this place," he said, and that tripped a switch in her memory. Jamie had once said that she wanted to hook up Megan with her boss, who was super hot. Jamie was right—Becker was smoking. "Speaking of, can I interest you in a beer? All locally brewed and all named after dog breeds. In addition to klutzes, I happen to be a big fan of dogs."

She laughed. "Dogs are cool. So's beer."

"We have wine, too, if that's your thing."

"And why on earth would I drink wine when you have microbrews named for dogs? How about a Chihuahua?" she said with a smile. "I'll take my chances even though I have no idea what kind of beer the Chihuahua gave its name to, but those are some seriously fine-looking little dogs."

"One raspberry ale coming up for the woman who doesn't like crowds, who thinks bras suck, and who believes owls have deeper meanings."

Whoa. In five minutes he already knew more about her than most people did. And she'd been trying so hard to keep everyone out.

Chapter Two

Perhaps retreat had its rewards after all. Look what it had brought tonight in the form of Megan. She was devastatingly beautiful and had a lush little body he could wrap his hands around, but looks alone had never done him in. The fact was, she had a dry sort of charm and a bit of an edge, like she was the kind of woman who didn't take shit from anyone. And there was something else, too. Almost a distance, as if she had walls up.

He understood walls. They made sense to him. They protected him from getting too close.

That's why he told Megan he owned the bar but said nothing of his work moonlighting as the local fire captain. It was the truth, but it also guaranteed she wouldn't be into him for the whole stereotype. He'd been there, done that, had an ex in Chicago who'd been far too interested in the job title and parading around the fireman she'd nabbed, like he was some sort of trophy. With Megan, he was Becker the bar owner, and he liked the fact that she was new to town, so there was no history, no expectations. She wasn't a local, so she thought of him only as maybe someone she wanted to spend the night with, because that's what he wanted, too. The way she'd said "Mr. Becker" sure as hell made him think about lifting her up and hitching those legs around his waist.

He walked quietly into the noisy bar and poured the beers, including a porter—dubbed the Great Dane—for himself. He returned to the back porch, drinking in the view along the way. The glow of the streetlamp along with the crescent moon bathed her face in soft light as she swiped a finger across the screen of her phone. He could tell she was reading a book rather than texting, and there was something hot about a woman who didn't need the distraction of checking her online status or sending emoticon-laden messages in a spare moment, but who instead chose the company of words to pass the time.

He joined her, and she tucked her phone away.

He handed her the beer. Their fingers touched, and she tilted her head, meeting his eyes. She didn't look away, just held his stare head-on, without shyness, without fear, and so he leaned closer to her and said, "To anti-crowds."

They clinked glasses.

"So you don't like crowds, but you own a bar. What's that all about?"

"Ironic, isn't it?" he said and raised one eyebrow playfully. Then he shifted to a more serious tone. "I'm fine with people. I just don't like scenes. But I like it when people are happy, and most people seem happy enough in a bar, especially this kind of a microbrewery in this kind of a town," he answered, giving her the simple truth. He might not have that kind of lightheartedness in his life, but he could serve it up. That was as close as he could get to it.

"And they're happy, but you're not with them." The noise of a busy evening of drinking filtered out, along with the sounds of the Black Keys on the bar's sound system, as Megan took a sip of the beer.

"So it seems."

"Do you wish you wanted to be a part of it, though? Do you wish you wanted to be in the middle of all that?" She leaned forward, waving her hand in the general direction of the Panting Dog, all while keeping her eyes fixed on him, as if she were keenly interested in his answers.

"Maybe someday," he said truthfully and was surprised at his ability to answer honestly. Not that he preferred lying; he simply preferred not answering. Only one person in town truly understood—his good friend Travis, not just because they played poker together every week and worked together on many shifts, but because Travis knew the same pain he did. He'd lost people close to him in the line of fire. Literally. They'd connected over that—a fireman's way of life, and a man's need to keep some things to himself.

But Megan's directness in asking him questions had an unexpected appeal. She seemed truly interested in knowing more, without needing to know everything.

"For now, you just escape from crowds?"

"Sometimes. It helps if there's a gorgeous woman who stumbles upon my back porch," he said, laying it out for her. To hell with holding back. He held so much inside, kept so many of his thoughts locked tight in his head. This was one he could set free.

"Lucky you," she said drily, but with a sexy glint in her

eyes.

"Am I? Lucky?" he asked, leaning closer, eager for her response.

She scoffed, but her expression was still playful. So was her body, as she crossed her legs, angling them nearer to him. Exactly where he wanted them to be. "Are you asking if you're getting lucky? 'Cause that's a bold question for so early in the evening," she said, her words seeming to suggest there would be a *later* to their evening.

"Trust me, I would never use a line like that and definitely not on a woman like you." He paused, looked her straight in the eyes, then added, "Unless it's later in the night."

"What *would* you use on a woman like me, then?" she asked, tracing her finger around the edge of her glass.

"I wouldn't use lines," he said confidently, never taking his eyes off her. He liked walls, but he didn't like games. "I would use words. All sorts of words. For now, I'd use direct ones. Tell me something about yourself, Megan."

"What do you want to know?"

As much as he was contemplating how she'd feel pressed up against him, he was curious about who she was beyond the owl tattoo and leather bracelet. He didn't need to know her plans for the future—hell, future was a four-letter word—but he wanted to know more about what mattered to her. Since she'd already mentioned her art, he'd go with that. "You're a freelance artist. What kind of art?"

"Want me to show you?" she asked, arching an eyebrow suggestively.

He had no clue what she was going to show him, but he liked her boldness. Heat rushed through his blood as she inched closer. "Yes," he said, swallowing thickly.

She reached inside her purse, rooting around till she grabbed a blue ballpoint pen. "Give me your hand, please."

He went along with it, offering her his open palm. She wrapped her slender fingers around his hand. Her touch was something he could get used to.

"I like to draw illustrations of animals, and I'm going to take your request now, sir," she said playfully.

He crinkled his brow, as if he were in deep thought. Truth was, he needed to devise a clever answer. If he said dog or cat, she'd probably thank him for the beer and be on her way. She liked to tango, to play, so he needed his request to be a good one. He wasn't going to ask for a snake or a lion. Nothing too obvious or tacky. He needed an animal that threw her off, made her think, made her laugh. Maybe an ostrich? How about a giraffe? Then he hit on it.

"I've always thought it a shame that they're not terribly domesticated because their masks are damn cute. So I choose raccoon," he pronounced.

"Raccoon masks are awesome," she said, then bent over his open hand. Her long hair inched dangerously close to his arm, the sweet, citrus scent of her shampoo permeating his senses. He toyed momentarily with the image of her head dropping farther and the things she could do in that position, but then he forced that thought away or else he'd be hard as a rock the rest of the night. Though he had been since he first saw her—he probably would be the whole night anyway.

She stopped drawing, wrapped his fingers into a fist to hide the graffiti, raised her head, and declared, "Done."

He opened his hand and burst out laughing. She'd drawn a cartoonish face of a raccoon, bandit mask and all, but then had circled him and penned a slash mark across the creature.

The words "Anti-Crowd Raccoon" were written underneath in bubbly ink.

"Our mascot," he quipped. "Maybe someday I can convince you to take it to the next level with the raccoon. Give him a proper body, turn him into a tattoo for me."

"Any time you're ready for a raccoon tattoo, you let me know."

"I'll hold you to that," he said, as he tapped her almost-empty glass. "Want more?"

"One's my limit. My ex was a total party boy. That's why I'm not into crowds."

"Oh yeah?"

"Yeah. He was an internet start-up guy. Entrepreneur type, but he basically blew all his money on—" She stopped and tapped the side of her nose.

"Glad to hear he's the ex, then. Not only because a woman like you doesn't need to be around that shit, but because it means you can be here with me tonight."

She smiled sweetly, and it was one of the first traces of softness he'd seen in her. She'd been like a good sparring partner so far, but now she showed a hint of vulnerability. Then she finished her glass. "And, as I said, I'm one and done."

"So is that it?"

She gave him a seductive look. "That's it for drinks…" She let her voice trail off.

"I take it you're open to other things?"

She shrugged with a grin. "What sort of other things?"

"This," he said, and stood up, pulled her from her chair, and put his hands on her cheeks. He looked deeply into her eyes, meeting her gaze, full of want. "I told you I'd be direct, and I've got my mind on kissing you right now."

"Do it," she said, confidence in her voice.

Damn, this woman knew what she wanted, and evidently, she wanted him.

He moved closer, capturing her mouth with his, sliding his tongue across hers. The first taste of her was intoxicating. She was sexy as sin; she didn't hide it and she didn't flaunt it, she just was it. She tasted like a woman who knew her mind, and knew her need, and wanted to be touched by him as much as he wanted to touch her.

She trembled against him, so he tugged her closer, letting her feel what it would be like if their bodies were aligned. She responded instantly, angling her hips against him as he crushed her delicious mouth. If you'd have asked him an hour ago what the chances were that he'd run into a gorgeous woman on his back porch, enjoy talking to her, and then tell her he planned to kiss her, he'd have scoffed.

Not because women were hard to come by, but because women like Megan didn't come around often, and as he kissed her more deeply, he was consumed with one thought—get her back to his place, strip her naked, and take his time getting to know every inch of her body. As he moved a hand down her side, she shivered and arched into him, her luscious lips pressing harder against his, the taste of her mouth heady. She didn't just let him lead, though. She grabbed the back of his head, her fingers diving into his hair, and kissed hard with a kind of fearless abandon, a confidence that was damn near dizzying and left his head foggy as the heat flared between them. The way their bodies responded to each other, it was as if this whole day, whole week, whole year had been leading up to this night, to the possibility of this sort of instant chemistry.

His hands found their way under her tank and up her chest. She breathed harder, moaning appreciatively as he cupped her breasts; they felt as good as they'd looked. Round, full, and real. He broke the kiss. "Glad that bra was giving you problems," he said in a low voice.

"Yeah?"

"You looked hot taking it off, and you feel amazing in my hands."

She answered him with another kiss. Hard, hungry, and devouring. He inhaled sharply as she raked her fingernails against his scalp, picturing how she'd twine those hands in his hair as he buried his face between her legs. As soon as the thought had touched down in his head, there was no room for anything else in his life right then. He pulled apart for the briefest of seconds. "I live two blocks away. Let me undress you. Let me spread you out on my bed. Let me taste you," he said in a low, raspy voice, his tone conveying his desire.

Her lips were parted and her eyes were filled with lust. "I'm just going to tell my friend I won't be meeting her," she said, sending a quick text, then turning her phone off. He liked that she powered it down. She could live in the moment, not in what she might be missing.

He didn't bother saying good-bye, or locking the back door, or grabbing anything from the Panting Dog. He had his wallet and his keys and the sexiest woman who'd come through Hidden Oaks in the whole year he'd been here. She was someone who didn't know who he was. Someone who didn't have the time for more than the here and now. With her, there was no past. There was only the present.

That was all he wanted, and all he was good for.

Chapter Three

Megan had never imagined last night when her brother pulled up in the driveway of their childhood home, dropping her off after having covered miles and miles of highway from Southern to Northern California, that she'd walk into the town square the next evening and find a man like this.

He was the type of man who made a woman nearly catcall like a construction worker. With a chest she could tell stories about for the rest of her life, every square inch of his body defined and cut, he could easily grace the pages of the fireman's calendar she'd start shooting in two days. The eye candy she'd never let herself have.

Wrapped up in each other in the entryway to his house, he kissed her deeply while skimming his hands down her back, racing over her hips, angling her close. His touch possessed an ownership to it, as if he could do things to her, take her places she'd never been. She ached between her thighs, desperate to know his body better. Running her hands across his gray T-shirt, her fingers mapped the perfect outline of his pecs, then his waist. "Do you have any idea how ridiculously perfect your body is?"

He smiled sweetly, then shook his head. "I don't want to talk about me. What I want is to see all of you." He nodded to the top of the stairs.

She kicked off her boots, not wanting to scuff the hardwood floors.

"Megan, I would have been totally fine if you left those on. Even if you scratched my floors, I wouldn't care," he said with a laugh. It was as if he could read her mind.

The house was dark, his home cast in shadows as they walked through the dining room, then the living room. But the dim light seemed fitting for tonight. She didn't even know his last name, and she was 100 percent okay with that. Darkness, namelessness, and his body pressed against hers were all she wanted right now.

He led her to his bedroom, to a king-size bed with a dark blue comforter and one lone pillow. There was a nightstand on each side of the mattress, but only one was brimming with books.

"Nice bed," she said.

"What would make this bed look really good is you on it," he said, and then lowered her to the soft comforter and ran his hand down her legs. She was grateful she'd shaved today; her legs were smooth and still faintly smelled of the vanilla-sugar lotion she'd smoothed on earlier tonight. "Your legs are spectacular," he said, with an appreciative groan as he trailed his hands along her skin.

"Why thank you. Now let's even things up a bit and get that shirt of yours off."

He reached for the underside of his T-shirt and started to remove it, but Megan held up a hand.

"Wait. I want to." She sat up and took over the T-shirt-removal reins, inching it up slowly, enjoying every moment of the reveal. As she reached his carved pecs, her fingernails trailing his skin led him to hitch in a breath. Then she tugged off the shirt. He was a beautiful sight indeed, made of the finest muscle, and skin, and hardness. A heady wave of anticipation rushed through her as she explored his chest thoroughly, her hands finding their way to his waist.

His perfect fucking waist dipped seductively into those jeans, hanging low on his hips. The best part was the way the pants couldn't mask how much he wanted her, too. She pressed a hand against his erection, narrowing her eyes and giving him a very knowing look as she felt how hard he was. Yes, this man wasn't just strong and tall; he was the whole package, including *the* package. Megan could tell he'd fill her in a way she'd never been filled before, and the image of him inside her was so powerful, so enticing, that she grabbed his shoulders and yanked him down on the bed with her. She wanted him to touch her, to feel what he'd done to her.

"Damn, woman. You're a feisty one."

"I'm a woman who knows what she wants," Megan said, and she did, especially now that she'd extracted herself from a bad relationship. She'd moved with her ex all the way to L.A., tied to the back of his entrepreneurial dreams and eager for a new adventure in Southern California, only to watch him turn into someone she no longer knew—an addict.

Their relationship had been unraveling over the last few months, which meant they hadn't had any moments like this. There had been no tangling of arms and legs and lips in the bedroom of their apartment. She'd laid down the law with him—there would be no coming together when he was high, and Jason had made it clear that he preferred that feeling to her. She'd tried so hard to help him get sober, to clean him up. But he loved a substance more.

After those last few painful months with him, she was finally free. She hadn't originally planned to come back here on her way to Portland, but right now, Megan was sure this night with Becker was one of the things she'd remember most fondly about her brief return to her hometown. One night without drama. One night with only pleasure. One hot night with Becker would erase all the bad. She danced her fingers across his sexy waist, the hard planes of his abs, enjoying his reaction as he drew a deep breath.

"And what do you want, Megan? Tell me what you want, and I'll give it to you."

"You. Inside me," she said, as she let go, then wrapped her legs around his waist. His reflexes were quick. He reached back with one arm, grabbing her calf and holding her tight, then rocking against her, showing her how he would take her. "Like this? You want me to take you like this?"

Her breath caught. "Yes."

"Then we'd better get your clothes off."

Megan started to unzip her skirt, but Becker shook his head. "Where are my manners? A woman like you—I'm not just going to fuck you. I'm going to pleasure every inch of you. I'm going to bury my face between those beautiful legs first. I'm not going to skip over that part."

She closed her eyes and gasped. God, she wanted that. She wanted that softness of his tongue, that delirious sensation of his lips on her. More than that, she wanted the letting go of control that came with that sort of touch, with this kind of man devouring her. She needed something that felt good and only good.

"Yes. That. I like that."

He raised an eyebrow. "Oh, you do?"

"Well, I think I might, but really, we're going to have to see, aren't we?"

"Challenge accepted," he said, as he pushed her skirt up to her waist, deftly removed her panties in one swift move, and placed his strong hands on the inside of her thighs, spreading her wide. His eyes blazed as he stared at her, so ready for him.

"I never come quickly, so let's see what you can do."

"That only makes me more determined to taste you coming on my tongue in less than a minute." Then he stopped talking, and his lips were on her, a rumbling sound from his throat saying he liked what he was doing. "So wet," he murmured, and the mood shifted, their playful banter disappearing, replaced by true need.

"I've been turned on since you first touched me," she said, letting go of the teasing because her obvious desire was the honest truth.

She was molten for him.

He swept his tongue through her wetness, kissing her so sensuously that the world narrowed to only this absolute pleasure he wanted to bring her. As she arched her back, he cupped her ass in his hands, tilting her hips closer to his face. He licked and kissed her, groaning hungrily, as if nothing else had ever tasted so good. Flicking his tongue against her swollen clit, he stroked her with a finger, and the twin sensations sent her soaring.

She gasped, her sharp breath turning into a long, low moan of desire. His mouth was out of this world. His tongue was epic. His touch was like nothing she'd ever felt before. Pressing his hands gently but firmly on the inside of her thighs, he spread her legs farther, and she let him, her knees falling open easily, offering him complete access with that magic mouth he possessed. She wanted to be vulnerable to him, to give her body to him, because he knew precisely what to do with her.

Her breathing grew more intense as he traced her with his skilled tongue, pressing against her clit at just the right moment, then sliding a finger inside her in a way that sent her to another plane of pleasure entirely.

To one that vibrated with bliss. That hummed with desire.

"That feels so good," she managed to say in between short breaths, and she was no longer playful, teasing Megan. She was the Megan who wanted to let go, who wanted to give in to pleasure, to the delicious sensation of not being in control. She wanted the connection, the closeness, the intensity of spreading herself open to him and letting him take charge of her pleasure.

"Don't stop, please don't stop," she said, because he was touching her perfectly, so perfectly that she repeated those words over and over as he tasted her, his mouth bringing her closer to the edge. As his tongue swept up her, circling in the most exquisitely intense motion, she could feel deep in her belly the start of release.

This never happened. She never came quickly. She was a marathoner, not a sprinter, and there were plenty of times when she was a non-finisher.

But now, as his mouth sent her hips arching, her voice

gasping, Megan had a feeling that she just might be doing the forty-yard dash. Becker's finger hit her in a way that made her dizzy with a new form of want. For the first time ever, she felt that wave of release in minutes, an orgasm she didn't have to work for, one that crashed over her as the intense shocks of pleasure from his tongue and his lips and his hands rocked through her body. She grabbed at his hair, pulling him even closer as she cried out.

She shuddered, flinging her hand over her face, because the feelings that raced through her body were too intense for her to make eye contact. She'd never felt this way before. She'd never been to this zone of bliss. Even though it was just sex—or foreplay, really—it also wasn't. She'd given herself to him in a moment of intense intimacy, writhing against his mouth, bucking under his tongue. She wanted more of it, more of him, more of this kind of connection.

As Megan moved her hand so she could look at him again, there was no denying the satisfied smile on his face. But there was something sweet there, too, in his dark eyes. He wasn't just a bang-on-my-chest-I-made-you-come guy. She could tell that a part of him was so damn happy that he'd done this for her. That he'd made her feel as if she had the best O of her life. Because she had, and he'd given it to her.

As promised. As advertised. In minutes.

"You can say I told you so," she said with a loopy sort of grin as she lay there, feeling spent.

Becker bent over her, straddling her. He brushed a finger tenderly against her top lip and met her gaze, the look in his eyes both intense and honest. "I would never say I told you so. I'm just glad you liked it. I'm glad I could make you feel good."

"I didn't like it. I loved it. I loved your mouth on me." She felt him through his jeans, loving the sheer hardness and length of him. "I want more of you," she whispered in a soft voice that went beyond the mere want she felt in her body. She *needed* him. More than she thought she would. She needed this man, and the way his touch was some kind of antidote to all that had gone wrong in the past. "I want to see you with your clothes off. I want to see all of you."

His dark eyes were blazing, and he licked his lips once, then planted a hard kiss on her mouth, grinding once against her thigh so she could have a tease of what he wanted to give her. She grabbed at his ass, pulling him against her.

"You keep saying and doing things like that, and it's not going to take me long. I want to savor you, because you deserve that kind of attention," he said, and Megan's heart threatened to sprint out of her body. He was a wizard with his tongue, a gentleman with his actions, and a swoon-maker with his words.

He moved off the bed, and seconds later, he returned with protection and started to unzip his jeans.

She sat up straight. "Let me."

He held out his arms, gesturing playfully to his pelvis.

"Come and get it," she said, as if she were providing the caption for a photo of him right now. Funny, how she could almost see him posing for a picture, poking fun at himself. He'd be a good subject with those eyes, that hair, that body.

"And then we'll both come."

She wiggled her eyebrows. "I can't think of a better idea than that," she said, reaching for the zipper and sliding it down, then pushing his jeans and briefs to the floor. She inhaled sharply as she caught sight of his cock for the first time. Beautiful, long, and thick.

His breathing intensified when she touched him. His eyes zeroed in on her. "Tell me something. Do you want me to spread you out on the bed? Take you on all fours? Bend you over? Or do you want to throw me down on the bed, climb on top of me and ride me into oblivion?"

She held up one finger. "I'll take one ticket on the ride to oblivion, please." She moved her hands to his hips and shoved him down on the bed. Megan laughed as he pretended to fall hard, like she'd truly slammed this big, strong man down on the bed.

Then her laughing faded, and so did his as she straddled him, and took the condom from his hand, and slid it on him. Heat spread through her body as she touched him, thrilling at his reaction and the way his cock throbbed in her hand.

She rubbed him against her entrance, and sparks flew through her body at that first exhilarating tease. Hardness against heat. Steely length against wetness. The look in his eyes—hazy, hungry—told her he craved all of her.

There was something so frighteningly intimate about this moment—the moment before. It was the anticipation, the thrill, the wonder, and the agonizing wish that she'd connect with this person the way she wanted. It was the hope that he'd feel as good inside her as her body believed, and her body was a member of the faithful. Every cell in her longed for him, and her blood rushed hot and fast through her veins.

But there was also something nerve-racking about having sex for the first time—whether she was fucking a stranger or making love to someone she knew. "Becker," she whispered urgently, suddenly feeling the need to say *this*. "I didn't go wandering behind your bar tonight looking for anything like this. I just want you to know that. But now it's all I want."

He grinned wildly, like she'd said the one perfect thing. "Then let's give you what you want, because I wasn't hanging out behind my bar scoping for action, but now you're all I can think about."

. . .

He locked eyes with her as she lowered herself onto him, her brown hair falling in a tumble across her naked shoulders, her body so hot and ready. Her lips parted, and she moaned so sexily that the sound alone sent the temperature in him soaring. Her reactions, her pleasure, her sighs as she moved on him were like a fucking symphony, a gorgeous sound that blotted out everything else in the world. He was a giver; he knew that about himself. He wanted to give pleasure more than he wanted to receive it. And while he had nothing whatso-fucking-ever against coming, his mission was to make her come again, and to hear a chorus of cries and shouts from her as he took her over the edge.

He palmed her bottom, moving her up and down. "You feel so good, Megan. I love the way you move on me."

"You're pretty fun to ride," she said, bending closer as she rocked up and down, her hot flesh gripping him, sending tremors throughout his body. Her breasts bounced lightly as she moved, and that was all the invitation he needed to fondle them. Besides, if he didn't have his hands on her breasts in this position, then he'd need to have his brain examined. He reached for them, kneaded her flesh and squeezed her nipples. Her breath caught as she closed her eyes, luxuriating, it seemed, in his touch.

"That's pretty much the fastest way to send me over the edge," she murmured.

"That is excellent intel to have. And thank God you got rid of that pesky bra earlier in the night."

"I think this is why you didn't resist having me on top," she said. "Better access to my breasts."

"You figured me out. Besides, resistance is futile," he said, rocking his hips into her with powerful thrusts. He stroked her nipples as he fucked her, and judging from her moans, she might have been ready to rocket into another climax. Yeah, that's exactly where he wanted to send her. He wanted to hear that beautiful music falling on his ears. He'd join her there soon enough; his climax was visible on the horizon now, coming into view as pleasure pulsed through his veins.

"Do you know what I thought when I first saw you? I thought you were stunning walking down the street. And now I know you're even more breathtaking when you come," he said, his voice hot and husky against her skin as he pulled her to him. He ran his hands through her hair. "And I want to see that again."

"You're going to," she panted, crying out in pleasure, the expression on her face absolutely decadent as her lips fell open. She rode him faster and harder until he felt her tighten around him, then dig her nails into his shoulders, holding on hard as she came undone on him.

Then he fucked her relentlessly through his own orgasm, until he collapsed alongside her, in that same state of delirium that strangers who were now lovers sought. He kissed her shoulder, her neck, her ear. There was a light sheen of sweat on her skin, and he found it made her all the more alluring. He stepped away for a minute to toss out the condom, and when he returned, he pulled her in close. "Thank you for coming home with me tonight," he whispered.

"Thank you for inviting me. You're amazing."

"So are you."

"We should do that again," she said, and he tensed momentarily at the prospect of more. A knee-jerk reaction, given his own relationship fears that ran so deep they needed their own running shoes. Then he tried to let go, reminding himself that she was safe because she wasn't even in town that long. "I mean, tonight. Or tomorrow. You know, before I leave town," she continued.

"When do you head out?"

"Soon. I'm here for a couple weeks."

Music to his ears. He wanted more of her. More of this. But not so much that he'd have to deal with the shit he couldn't handle. A few weeks was finite. A few weeks meant an end. It wasn't that he was averse to commitment. He just knew it wasn't in any woman's best interests to be committed to *him*.

"Then why don't we do this again tomorrow night? How about around, say, ten p.m. you walk into my alley and take off your underwear. I'll act like a gentleman like I don't see it—"

She smirked and swatted his arm. "But in reality, you'll be watching every little bit of my alley striptease."

"Of course. I'm a man. A beautiful woman walks by, it would be wrong of me to look away."

"You want a repeat tomorrow night? I'll shimmy out of my panties."

He grew hard again with the images that flashed before him, and he pulled her closer, wrapping her up in his arms. She fit there well. "Mmm. Yes, then give them to me, and I'll find a way to shield you from prying eyes as I make you come again."

"I believe that could be arranged."

Soon, she was snuggling in closer, and he didn't mind, not one bit. In fact, he had the best night of sleep in ages.

Chapter Four

She didn't want to wake him up. The man looked so damn peaceful, as if he was deep in dreamland. She quietly ripped out a sheet of paper from her notebook and wrote her number on it, then drew a quick picture of a raccoon.

A very female, very sexy raccoon with curvy hips and a trim waist. She grinned at the image. It felt like a private little joke — their shared thing. She considered it and decided it needed an article of clothing, so she added a bra, and in the middle of the bra she wrote her number.

Text me sometime.

She made her way to the door, stopping briefly in the kitchen for a glass of water. She scanned the room quickly, hunting for glasses in a dish rack so she wouldn't need to go rooting through his cupboards. There was a newspaper stacked on the kitchen table, with one section removed. How quaint that he still had a paper delivered. Or maybe

he didn't read it, judging from the way the paper looked untouched and unread.

She noticed the section spread out was the comics, and
she laughed. Okay, that was kind of adorable. She peered
closer, looking for *Calvin & Hobbes*, since that strip had
been a favorite of hers and Travis's since they were kids.
Then she saw that he wasn't reading this section for the fun-
nies. He'd completed the crossword puzzle.

In. Pen.

Damn, the guy was smart, too?

There went her heart, with a little flutter.

She turned away from the table and headed for the sink.
The counter was neat and organized, with just a pile of mail
next to a box of Cinnamon Life cereal. She felt a surge of
giddiness. Cinnamon Life was her favorite, too.

Okay, it's just cereal.

Besides, it was the way he talked to her and seemed gen-
uinely interested in what she said that she liked the most.
She smiled to herself. Yep. This was going to be a lovely
little fling. In one fantastic night, he'd already proven a delicious antidote to putting Jason and their botched history
behind her. A few more romps, and she'd eradicate all those
cruel memories. She reached for a glass from next to the
sink, poured herself some water from the tap, and finished
it quickly.

She walked home as the sun rose, pink streaks leaking
across the sky, waking it up. Tingles raced through her chest
at the memory of how she'd spent the last night. So unexpected. So hot, and yet so tender in some ways, too. This was
only a brief encounter, something to pass the time during
her short stay here. But what a way to pass the time with a

man who'd made her laugh, then made her cry out his name.

It had a quick beginning, it would have a brief middle, and then a perfect, painless end when she picked up one more time and left.

Megan hummed a tune as she watered the flowers in her mother's front yard later that morning after she and Becker had exchanged a few sexy text messages. The newest Jane Black song was playing in her head, a sexy number about new lovers, so it seemed fitting for her to hum as she gave the tiger lilies a little something to drink. When she stopped, she stood back to consider one of the fiery orange flowers, its long petal looking like the tongue of a rock star. She tilted her head to the side, picturing that petal adorning a shoulder blade, a forearm, maybe even a hip. That would make for a cool design for a tattoo. Later that afternoon, once she and Jamie went to the olive oil fair in the town square, she'd sketch it out.

"Look at you. Up early, watering Mom's plants, just like old times. Did you already bake muffins and scrub the floors, too, like a perfect little house sitter?"

Megan swiveled around and beamed at Travis. She wrapped her arms around him in a hug, even though she'd seen him earlier in the week on the drive to Hidden Oaks; all her belongings, including her motorcycle, had been loaded into the bed of his truck.

"You know I'm allergic to any chores that don't require the use of my very green thumb," she joked as they pulled apart, and she set down the watering can. "But I do love to garden."

"Nice to see you here taking care of the plants again." He leaned against the porch railing. "Did you have a nice time last night?"

Red rushed across her cheeks. "Sure," she muttered, and she resumed watering so he wouldn't see the guilty look in her eyes. Not that she'd done anything wrong by hooking up with Becker, but Travis surely didn't need to know she'd gotten busy her first night back in town. Travis never liked the guys she went out with. The typical older brother, he didn't ever think anyone was good enough for his sister, and he surely wouldn't think well of a man she'd slept with after one hour of knowing him.

"You saw Jamie at the Panting Dog, right?"

She nodded as she watered. "Yes," she said, then immediately her chest tightened. She hated lying to him. "No, I mean. It was too crazy in there, Trav. I just sat out back in the alley and read a book."

Fine, so that wasn't the truth, either. But it bore a semblance to the truth.

"Ah, you're such a good girl, keeping your nose in books and staying out of trouble," he joked. Then he narrowed his eyes. "You aren't getting into any trouble while you're back in town, are you?"

Megan scoffed. "Please."

"Well?"

"What sort of trouble would I get into in one day back in Hidden Oaks? I'm going to the olive oil fair with Jamie in a little bit."

"I mean things like skipping school to hang out by the river. Skinny-dipping in the waterfall. Making out with some boy behind Jamie's parents' vineyards," he said, recounting her high school antics.

"Trav," she chided. "I'm not seventeen anymore."

He roped his arm around her neck and gave her a noogie. "Doesn't matter. You'll always be my baby sister, and it's my job to keep you out of trouble."

"You need to stop worrying about me," she said, but she knew that was a futile request.

He'd always worried and had always protected her, stepping into the role of "man of the house" when their firefighter father had died. She'd been six, and Travis had been ten.

Her mom had been devastated for years over their father's death, broken and hobbled by grief. He'd saved a family in a fire, but when he went back for one of his men, the home collapsed under the flames, pinning him beneath a burning beam. Megan hadn't just lost a dad; she'd lost her mom for a time, too. She and Travis had grown up fast—the two of them together taking care of laundry, meals, and cleaning the house on the days their mom could barely make it out of bed.

Finally, years later, her mom had surfaced again. But she didn't truly move on until she met and married a guy who ran a bookstore. There weren't very many hazards to life and limb when you peddled books—a fact that her mom had pointed out numerous times to Megan's brother when he decided to take up the mantle of their dad and add volunteer firefighter to his credentials. Her mom had argued and battled and bargained to try to keep Travis out of the firehouse, telling him his moonlighting job playing and teaching poker was all he needed, but had no such luck.

Travis was a gambler, and fire was in his blood.

In Megan's, too. The aversion to it, at least. She had no intention whatsoever of following in her mom's footsteps, and that's why firefighters were eye candy only to her. That's all they'd be for the next week as she shot the calendar, especially since she had real candy in the form of one very sexy bar owner.

"Want to get a cup of coffee?" Travis offered. "I'm meeting up with some of the guys from the firehouse. Smith is probably bringing Jamie along," he said.

"Sure."

"All right, let's go, Miss Megan. There's a great coffee shop a block away from the firehouse. McDoodle's has the best coffee in Northern California. Maybe you've heard of it."

She rolled her eyes. "Stop it. You know I love McDoodle's. I used to live here, you know."

"Yeah, and you act like you've never set foot in this town."

If he only knew how much acting she'd done last night. She'd never even told Becker that she was from here and that she knew this town inside and out.

Maybe because she liked the idea of not settling down anywhere.

Chapter Five

Becker finished the day's crossword puzzle in twenty minutes flat. It was damn near a record for him, but he wasn't surprised. Puzzles made him focus on the simple action of thinking about clues, rather than about people. Puzzles kept his brain trained on the present, so he wouldn't linger in the past.

But this distraction was done, and he didn't have a new one handy. When he put down the pen, his mind instantly tripped back in time, revisiting that punishing loop in his head of one night last year when everything was lost. He ran through all the things he could have done differently. *If I'd moved faster. Turned sooner. Grabbed harder.* As if that would change anything. Still, hitting replay had become a habit for him, and one he showed no signs of kicking.

Memories flashed by, and he let them crash over him.

A frigid night in Chicago. A crackling on the scanner. A 911 call had come from a condo downtown. Candles left burning had toppled over, and just like that, the entire top floor of the building was consumed. He could still hear the hiss of the flames if he listened hard enough. Could see the wall toppling. Pain sliced though him, like it was happening right now as his hands couldn't hold on to his men. As he watched them take their last breaths.

That's why he hadn't wanted to be toasted for doing his job here in Hidden Oaks, when he'd rescued two kids a few weeks ago from a fast-moving fire that tore through the second story of an old house down at the end of a quiet lane. His name and Travis's had been plastered all over the local news and radio, declaring them heroes. But that wasn't what the job was about. It wasn't about the attention, or the congrats, or any of that. He'd do what he did if no one noticed, if no one came by, if no one thanked him. Because it could go either way. Sometimes you saved the people you needed to save; sometimes you lost them.

He folded the paper, slapping it down on the stack, recalling his conversation with Travis about the way the job could dig into you, how losses could stick with you. That was what they signed up for. They knew the costs. But those nights, those calls—no matter the outcome—had a way of latching onto you, of claiming some ownership to your brain or your heart. Given how things had gone in the last year, there was a lot of real estate in him that was already staked. He honestly wasn't sure how much was left for the taking.

He glanced over at his phone on the table, as if it were a reminder of the good things in life. The moments that didn't hurt. Like last night with Megan. He could recall perfectly the taste of her, the smell of her, but more than that—all of her. She'd been a fiery lover, daring and direct. She'd told him what she wanted, she'd challenged him, and he had risen to the task and then some. She'd shown a vulnerable side, too, that drew him in, like the way she let go and shared parts of herself. Add in that quirky sense of humor, and she was exactly what he'd needed. He picked up his phone and texted her. He could write something dirty, something romantic, or something direct about seeing her tonight. But she'd left him a drawing of a raccoon wearing a bra, so he went in a different direction.

I see our mascot is a bit of a nudist.

A few minutes later, she replied. *It's fun being naked.*

Then a second text arrived. *With you.*

And just like that, he was hard again. *You should get naked with me again tonight.*

Another answer. *I will. :)*

Ah, now some things were just nice and easy. Like connecting with her. She eased his mind.

With a grin on his face, he grabbed his keys and wallet from the counter, then headed to the local coffee shop a few blocks away.

He rounded the block and saw that the line at McDoodle's was long. He took his post and started running through his plans for the next few days. Tomorrow, he was meeting the photographer at the firehouse, so before then he'd go for a long morning run. Running was his therapy. It let him clear his head as best he could so the pain didn't clutch him like a vise. Running could do wonders to numb a brain. So he'd run some more tomorrow, then the next day, then the next...

"Let me guess. You're going to take a coffee. Black. No

sugar."

It was Smith Grayson. Becker turned around, grateful for the distraction. Smith, also a volunteer fireman, was always in a good mood. Becker often wished he could siphon a little bit of that off, use it for himself.

"Let me guess. You're going all frothy and getting something with caramel and sugar in it," Becker said.

Smith smiled broadly. "We can't all be stoic and go for the no-frills drinks." Then he added, "But I'm here to get a latte for the lady."

"Right. You just pretend the caramel mocha frappa treat-o you order is for Jamie."

Smith and Jamie had hooked up at the Spring Festival last month, and it had been about time. It had been obvious to him and anyone else with a pulse that they were hot for each other. Now they were nearly inseparable, and deeply in love.

"As a matter of fact, I'm not pretending. She's out walking the dog, and is going to join me here soon. And she was saying an old friend of hers she was supposed to see last night is meeting us here any minute now, too."

Becker's ears pricked at the last few words: *supposed to see last night.*

What were the chances?

"Yeah? Where's this friend from?" He reached the counter and was greeted by one of his favorite ladies in Hidden Oaks, Mrs. McDoodle, a longtime Hidden Oaks resident who'd taken a shine to Becker after he arrived in town last year. There was something very no-nonsense about the sturdy, gray-haired woman. She worked hard, ran a solid business, and took care of her customers. Becker could appreciate that kind of workmanlike approach to life.

"Hi, handsome, what'll it be for you? The usual?" She smoothed her hands over the once-white, now coffee-stained apron.

"Cup of joe. Straight up. And whatever my friend here wants," Becker said as he pointed to his buddy.

Smith placed a hand on his heart, as if he were overcome with emotion at the gesture. "Oh my, Becker. Aren't you the nicest fella in the world to pay for my drinks."

"Watch it. Or I'll rescind the offer."

"One latte. Two-percent milk. With room for cream," he said. Smith leaned closer to Mrs. McDoodle and whispered in a low voice, but one Becker could still hear. "And a hot chocolate for me, okay? Whipped cream and all the works. Even those little chocolate shavings."

Mrs. McDoodle winked and went to work. A minute later, she served the drinks, pushing them across the counter to Becker.

"How's that old Ford running?" Becker asked, since he helped her with her car from time to time. He might not have family here in Hidden Oaks, but he'd become a part of the community through the bar, through his work, and by helping out when he could. That had all gone a long way to making Hidden Oaks a true home.

"It's a little shaky. Kind of rumbles a bit when I idle at lights."

"Want me to come by and take a look?"

"I would love that," she said and beamed at him.

He saluted her playfully. "It's a date, then. Tomorrow."

He joined Smith at the end of the counter as his buddy added a little bit of half-and-half to the latte. Becker took a swallow of his coffee, then returned to the thread of their conversation. "So you said Jamie has a friend back in town," he prompted, wondering if somehow that friend was Megan. She'd seemed like a wanderer, breezing through town, hitching a ride on some sort of star in the distant sky. Even the way she vanished this morning, leaving a sexy-flirty little note as he slept, felt sort of like a dream. Then he remembered he didn't even know where she hailed from. Could Megan somehow be friends with Jamie?

Smith nodded. "Oh yeah. Apparently they go way back. All the way to high school and before. They were supposed to see each other last night, but I guess something came up, so Jamie was pretty much bouncing with excitement when she was getting ready this morning. She can't wait to see Megan."

Ah, so Megan was a local. Interesting that she hadn't mentioned being from here. Interesting too that she was friends with his employee.

"I just hope Travis doesn't monopolize all Megan's time. He's super close to his sister."

Becker nearly choked on the hot liquid that burned his throat. "What did you say?"

"Travis is super close with Megan."

His brain froze, and he was sure all the systems in his body had stopped working. He was desperately searching for a way to rewind time, to erase what Smith said, to replace it with something else. Because there was no way that Megan could be Travis's sister, right? She'd said she was *just passing through*. She'd never said she was from here. Maybe there were two Megans. After all, Megan was a common name. Besides, Travis barely used his sister's name, usually referring to her, quite simply, as "my sister."

"The one who's going to shoot the calendar?" Becker asked in a stilted voice. His Megan had said she planned to be a tattoo artist. She'd never said a word about photographing firemen. He held on to the slim hope that the Megan he had planned to spread out on his bed again tonight and the Megan who shared the same last name as Travis weren't one and the same.

Smith nodded. "Yup. She's a good photog, Jamie says. Good artist too. She can draw pretty much anything, Jamie was telling me."

The possibility of two Megans went poof.

As the harsh reality set in, his stomach plummeted to the ground, then free-fell another several hundred feet. He'd had sex with his good friend's little sister last night, with one of his closest buddies' completely off-limits sister. Amazing, mind-blowing sex that he wanted more and more of.

He worked with Travis. Fought fires with Travis. Played poker with the man. Travis came from the same stock as Becker. Knew pain, knew hardship, knew guilt.

When he looked up, he spotted Megan walking through the door of the coffee shop—right next to her brother.

Chapter Six

Everything slowed, like the warbling of a record played at the wrong speed. Out of tune and too hard to make out.

The floor of the coffee shop felt wobbly as Travis made the introduction. She dug her toes in, gripping the floor like she was on a tram taking a curve at high speed.

"And this is the one and only Miss Megan," he said proudly, gripping her shoulder. "My amazingly talented sister who's going to shoot our calendar. And this is my fire captain, Becker Thomas."

Megan willed her cheeks not to flush, urged herself to keep the sheer and utter surprise coursing through her body from showing. She couldn't let on, *wouldn't* let on.

Be impassive.

Becker extended a hand to shake, and her mind flashed back to last night, to them shaking hands, then to all the places where his hands had been. In her hair, on her hips, between her legs as he spread her thighs wide open for his mouth.

Her insides were jumpy, and it was half from the shock and half from the delicious memories.

"Nice to meet you, Megan Jansen," he said, keeping his eyes locked on her, as if he'd caught her in a lie. She hadn't lied, though; she simply hadn't offered up a last name. There'd been no need to. Just like he hadn't mentioned being a fireman.

"Nice to meet you, *fire captain*," she added sharply, but he didn't let go of her hand. She didn't let go, either. For a brief moment, the clock stopped ticking, and in that stitch in time her mind was bursting with images from last night, her body flooded with the recall of the most delicious sensations they'd shared. Their eyes remained locked on each other, and she was sure he was seeing and feeling everything too. A shiver dared to race down her spine.

He dropped her hand, and she brushed her palm against her thigh, wishing she were anywhere but here.

Being near him was too damn difficult.

Minutes later, the five of them were outside the coffee shop, seated at a table, with Jamie's German shepherd puppy at her feet. Thank God for the dog—the adorable creature was the perfect distraction from the awkwardness of sitting across from her brother's boss whom she'd screwed last night. Not to mention rode, came hard on, and made plans to saddle up again.

Her head pounded. Maybe her brain was annoyed with her body's decisions.

"Chance is such a good boy," Megan said, stroking the little dog's head.

Jamie beamed. "He is, isn't he? I love him madly. We've been doing dog training lessons with Cara. You remember her, Megan? She's amazing."

"Wait. I thought it was all *my* superior training skills that made Chance into the perfect pet," Smith said jokingly, and Chance looked up, his tongue lolling out of his mouth, his tail wagging slightly.

Megan forced a laugh, then caught Becker's gaze once more. He looked back at her, those dark brown eyes connecting with her, full of unsaid things. She wanted to know if he felt as uncomfortable as she did, if he felt guilty. But she couldn't read him, and she swore she saw the slightest touch of anger in his eyes.

"You know," Travis began, "since the dog is so well-trained, maybe he should be in one of the pictures in the calendar. What do you think?" He directed the question to Megan.

"Sure," she said quickly.

Travis looked to Becker. "You like the idea?"

He simply nodded, but still kept his focus on Megan. For a second there, Travis glanced from Becker to Megan, then Megan to Becker, before he returned to the conversation. They chatted more about dogs, and the calendar, and the plans for the shoot. But the words were all mush in her head, because she was at war inside—hot memories swamped her brain at the same time as the shock over what she'd done.

She pushed her chair away.

"Excuse me for a minute."

She headed inside to the ladies' room, turned on the water, and splashed a cold stream of it on her face. She turned off the faucets, took a deep breath, then grabbed a paper towel to dry her cheeks.

Get it together, she told herself. She was going to be professional and cool. She couldn't let one mind-blowing night—which was a mistake—cloud her head. She left the bathroom and startled when she found Becker waiting in the hall.

"Why didn't you tell me you were from here?" he asked, holding his hands out in question.

She furrowed her brow. "What?"

"I had no idea you were Travis's sister," he said, and he sounded pissed.

"And I had no idea you were a fireman," she said, parking her hands on her hips.

He shoved a hand roughly through his hair, shook his head. "And I had no idea you were the photographer. You said you were an artist."

"I am!" she said, her voice rising. *What the hell?* "I *can* draw, and I do tattoos. I also happen to be good at shooting pictures. Besides, you said you were a bar owner," she pointed out, as if they could both redo this colossal mistake by rehashing the moments they both could have been more honest. "Why didn't you tell me more about yourself?" she countered.

He didn't answer. He moved closer, maybe a foot away now. The anger felt like a pulsating life force, but there was something else between them, too. *Heat.* And *want.* The nearness was intoxicating. She could reach out and touch his chest. That broad, sturdy chest that she'd loved having her hands all over.

She was edgy now, nervous, as they stood like two sparring partners, tucked away in the back hallway of the coffee shop near the restrooms. She wanted him to touch her again, and she hated that she was still thinking of last night, and how they'd connected so deeply in bed. But also in their conversations all through the night and up to a few minutes ago when they were texting. She was torn between needing to leave and wanting him to pin her against the wall and bury her in kisses that made her weak in the knees.

Too bad she could never do any of those things with him again.

. . .

He didn't tell her more because he didn't tell *anyone* more about himself. Because he liked it that way. Because he needed it that way. Pieces of the truth were easier to swallow than the whole truth—letting someone in meant the potential for pain, and he was looking for ways to ease the ache of the memories that choked him.

But even when he hadn't told her everything, even in those moments when he'd given her a sliver of his true self, he'd felt lighter that he had in ages. Being with her had felt... freeing. Maybe because she had a restless heart, and a carefree spirit, and he wanted a taste of that.

Rather than keep up the rapid-fire questions, he relented and let down his guard ever so briefly as he answered her honestly. "Because it was easier to just have you know a little bit," he admitted.

He was ready for her to lash out, to accuse him of not practicing full disclosure or something. Instead, she reached out her arm, grasped his forearm in her hand, gave him a squeeze. "Why is it easier?"

"Sometimes you just want to be able to only offer a part of yourself," he said, almost surprised that he was speaking so plainly, but glad too that he was able to say *that* much.

Her brown eyes were kind, understanding even, as the corner of her lips curved up briefly. "I know what you mean.

I'm usually pretty up-front and open. But sometimes it's easier not to give the whole résumé."

He glanced down at her hand on his arm and swallowed. His throat was dry. That simple contact made him want more of her, made him crave that night they were supposed to have tonight. But she was so far off-limits now, she might as well be in another country.

"Yeah, sometimes it is," he said softly.

"I kind of wish I'd known who you were, but I guess I'm glad I didn't," she whispered.

"Same here," he said, and fought every instinct that told him to step forward, to pin her with his arms, to kiss her softly and tenderly, to savor the feel of her, the soft slide of her tongue, the gentle press of her body. He clenched his fists, digging his fingers into his palms to hold himself back from touching. He couldn't risk it. He couldn't chance his friendship with Travis. He'd already lost a good friend—he didn't need to add another. "But we can't see each other tonight."

"Obviously."

"Or any other night when you're in town."

"Definitely," she said and when they heard footsteps, she dropped her hand from his arm in a flash. "I'd better go."

Travis rounded the corner and stopped in his tracks, glancing curiously from Becker to Megan. "Well, I'm glad to see you two are getting to know each other. It'll make for a better shoot. Now, if you'll excuse me," he said and pointed to the restroom.

• • •

As the woman he absolutely would never touch again left

the coffee shop on her way to the town square with Jamie, the little dog gamely leading the way, Travis hung back and pulled Becker aside. "Saw you and my sister chatting."

"Yeah," Becker said, clearing his throat. "We were just talking about the calendar."

The lie gnawed at his chest, like a weed twisting in him.

"Just make sure things stay focused on the calendar when she starts tomorrow."

Becker shot him a curious look, narrowing his eyes. The weed dug deeper. "Of course."

"Good. Because I saw the way you two were looking at each other, Beck. She was checking you out, and you were checking her out. I trust you with my life, man, but you gotta stay away from her. You know you're not in a place to give my sister the relationship she deserves."

Becker stopped walking, held up his hands. "Whoa. Let's not put the cart before the horse. I'm not looking for any sort of relationship."

Relationships meant closeness, they meant intimacy, they meant the possibility of caring deeply about another person. But in an instant, you could be gone. Relationships meant the slow start of the end of things. That was the only way attachments ever went.

"I know," Travis said emphatically. "And just keep it that way when it comes to her. She's only in town for a few weeks and she just got out of a shitty deal with her ex. Just keep it all on the up and up."

"Trav, nothing is going to happen. I assure you," he said, and willed himself to mean it. He cloaked himself with his game face, while inside he reeled with worry over how his friend would react if he knew. Would Travis blacklist him?

He didn't know and didn't want to know.

Travis clapped him on the back. "Good. That's what I want to hear. Or else I'd have to…" He let his voice trail off as he cracked his knuckles, adopting a menacing glare. His voice was light, though, and Becker knew it was a joke.

But even so, there was definitely a kernel of truth to this ribbing. There were codes, there were lines, and he certainly didn't need to cross them again.

Even though the crossing had been the best thing he'd had in ages, the only thing that had felt purely good.

Chapter Seven

"Pancakes! Who wants to bet I serve the most pancakes?"

Travis brandished a quarter, slipping it back and forth between his fingers. He was always betting on something or other. Usually the bets were much bigger and involved straights and flushes at executive card games he played all across wine country, in darkened rooms filled with cigar smoke and plenty of high rollers, made rich off vines and land. This morning, the bet was over which man from the shift would rack up the longest line and serve the most flapjacks at this morning's fund-raiser at a nearby hospital.

Just your average day at the Hidden Oaks Fire Department. The work here was more focused on responding to medical emergencies, hosting blood drives, and conducting fire safety classes at local schools than it was about fighting fires. The sleepy little wine country town was mostly nonflammable, though the blaze a few weeks back had been an exception.

Becker hadn't planned on joining the fire department when he'd moved here a year ago. He'd packed up his home in Chicago for Hidden Oaks because he needed a change. Hidden Oaks had been the perfect place for a new start. His financial adviser knew of an old pool hall in the middle of town that was prime real estate to be turned into a hip new bar. Becker signed the deal for the space that became the Panting Dog, and Hidden Oaks became his new home. For the first few months, he zeroed in solely on the bar.

But the lure of the firehouse proved too powerful to resist. It was a way of life. A calling, and so when the Hidden Oaks fire captain moved to Big Sur, Becker was offered the post. This town was much quieter than Chicago, which suited him just fine.

The trouble was he hadn't eradicated the painful memories of the fire in Chicago just by moving away. They still clung to him like a film and showed no signs of abating. The what-ifs were relentless. He hated to admit it, but sometimes he wondered if maybe he should quit the firehouse. Maybe he'd never get his head screwed on straight. Every now and then, he flirted with the idea of being just Becker the bar owner. Maybe that's why he liked being with Megan so much, because when he was simply the guy in the alley behind the Panting Dog, he wasn't carrying around a shitstorm of guilt.

But he wasn't a coward, and the thought of quitting ignited a fresh wave of shame. He didn't want to be that guy. He wanted to be someone who could deal, who could manage, who could rise above.

Fortunately, today's shift was all about pancakes and the calendar, and he damn well better be able to handle those two things.

"Is this even a contest?" Smith said as he strutted across the concrete floor, heeding the siren call of Travis's challenge. "You know I'm winning hands down, and you're going to be washing my truck for the next year."

"You're on," Travis said.

"And I'm betting that neither of you serves the most," Becker chimed in, trying to keep the mood light. "And you can put me down for heads or tails on that one."

"Who are you betting on, then, boss?" Travis asked.

"Anyone else. Anyone else but you two peacocks. Now get out of here."

"Aunt Jemima, here I come," Travis said as they strolled to the red truck parked outside.

The other guys on shift were upstairs, so Becker was effectively alone in the firehouse, and immediately thoughts of Megan descended upon him. He was gripped by the memory of her beautiful body, of the soft skin of her thighs, of the way she'd finally let down her tough-but-playful guard when he was buried between her legs. She was so vulnerable then as she'd arched into him, her spine bowing, her hair spread out across a pillow, her hands grappling in his hair. He could get lost in her touch, in pleasing her, in bringing her to the edge of desire again. The way she responded to him, to his lips, his mouth, his touch, was both an intense turn-on and also a balm to the loop that played too often in his head. When he was with her, there was nothing else in his head but her.

Pleasing her had made him feel good. Made him feel great, even. Like a painkiller that numbed all the noise. He wanted to go back there, to lose himself in her.

He pushed a rough hand through his hair.

He'd have to run for ten miles tomorrow to get that woman out of his mind, especially since she'd be here soon to go over the calendar. But daily tasks would do the trick for now, so he went through his usual morning routine of checking the equipment on the engine and making sure everything was in its proper place, until he heard the rumbling sound of a motorcycle pulling into the parking lot of the station.

He walked over to the open garage door and took in the sight before him. The motorcycle being parked. The kickstand knocked to the concrete by a black leather boot, and a woman dismounting the bike she'd been straddling.

He leaned against the wall, curious to watch. He was enjoying the view 100 percent and then some. Especially when the woman took off her helmet, shook out her hair once, twice, and a cascade of thick chestnut hair fell past her shoulders.

Of course.

Of course the owl-tatted girl rode a bike. She reached into the small storage space on the back of the bike and removed a sturdy navy-blue bag, and slung it over her shoulder. She gave him a curt wave, then glanced around the firehouse, maybe looking to see who else was there. Only him, and when it registered, she flashed a sweet smile as she walked up.

"Hey," she said softly, and that one word was like a reminder that they'd shared something more the other night.

"Hey, Megan. Or should I call you Miss Megan?" he asked, picking up on Travis's nickname for her.

"Please don't call me Miss Megan. It took me long enough to train him off using both names. You know he used to call me by my middle name too when I was younger?"

"What's your middle name?"

"Megan Margaret. He thought it was the height of hilarity — don't ask me why — to call me Miss Megan Margaret. Made me crazy."

"Why?"

"It's so looonnnng," she said, stretching out the word. "And it's so proper. Miss Megan Margaret is for a woman who goes to finishing school, who wears white gloves and jaunty hats and goes sailing."

He laughed. "I take it you don't wear jaunty hats?"

She patted her head as if looking for a hat. Then shook her head. "Nope. But I do like to draw jaunty hats on tigers or giraffes."

"Well, of course," he said, not wanting to let go of the thread of the conversation, of how they'd somehow slid right back into the chatter that had marked their Friday night. He leaned against the side of the truck, and she followed suit. They were facing each other. "So if Miss Megan Margaret wears gloves and goes sailing, then Megan rides a bike and plans to be a tattoo artist?"

Her eyes widened, and she brought her finger to her lips. "Shhh…"

"Travis and Smith are out at a pancake breakfast and the other guys are upstairs. It's just you and me."

"I know, but still. I haven't told him that. I haven't really told anyone the details even though it's been my dream."

His lips curved in a small smile. "But you told me. At least a little bit," he said softly, remembering how she'd said "someday soon" so wistfully when she talked about the opportunity to turn her drawings into body art.

"Yeah, I guess I did. I just found out that day that I landed an apprenticeship at a shop in Portland. Travis knows I'm going to Portland, but I haven't told him yet about the job and how much I've wanted it. I think he figures if I don't have a job he can convince me to stay here." She met his eyes. Hers were wide, with a hint of vulnerability. "And there I go again. Telling you my hopes and dreams."

"I like hearing them," he said softly.

They weren't touching; they were simply talking, but somehow this conversation was starting to feel as intimate as spending the night together. In both the things they'd held back and the things they'd shared—then and now—there was something between the two of them. A magnetic pull, maybe. Something that started with chemistry but was now turning dangerously close to...*interest.*

"I guess I like talking to you," she admitted in a low voice.

"I like that, too," he said, his gaze locked on hers. Her brown eyes met his, and she didn't look away. Her lips parted ever so briefly, and she took a deep breath. Tension rolled through him as he held back, as he fought every instinct to step closer, to touch her cheek, her shoulder, to run his hand down her arm.

To learn more about her. He could see this playing out in his mind. They'd talk more, he'd ask her why she liked to draw, he'd learn more about this woman who already fascinated him. Then he'd thread his fingers through her hair, leaning in slowly, torturously close to her delicious earlobe. Her scent would fill his nostrils, the sweet, sexy smell of her citrus-y shampoo, and then her—her hair, her skin, her heat. He'd brush his lips gently against her neck, and she'd mold her body to his. He'd grasp her wrists, backing her up against the red cab of the truck, her hips jutting out invitingly. Kissing her more, exploring her mouth, her lips, her neck.

The air was so thick and heady, the desire for this moment to become *more* intense, that he had to recalibrate. He snapped out of the fantasy. *Focus. She's Travis's sister. She's the calendar photographer. She's leaving town. She's not the woman you were going to enjoy several more nights with.*

"So," he said, clearing his throat and tapping the side of the truck. "The calendar."

She nodded several times. "Right. Right."

She fixed her lips in a straight, sharp line and focused her attention on her camera bag, rooting around in a side pocket. She removed a notebook, flipped it open, and tapped the page. "I looked at the last few calendars, and I definitely think there's some truth to the old adage 'if it's not broke, don't fix it.' And whatever you gentlemen did worked—women loved the calendar."

"Yep. I wish I could take some of the credit, but I wasn't even in last year's."

"That's clearly going to change this year, and women are going to be very excited to get their hands on your picture."

He laughed off the compliment. "I hardly think so."

"Becker," she said in a soft voice. "You're the most beautiful man at this firehouse."

His heart thumped harder, and so did other parts. "Thank you."

"Of course, that's purely my professional opinion as a photographer," she quickly added.

"Professional or personal, I'll take either one."

"But I want to up the ante a bit with this year's. I think there are a few more locations and looks we can try. I'd love to get some outdoor shots, not just ones Photoshopped with flames in the background, and maybe even do a little something with makeup, sort of makeup on the chest, to connote smoke. Let me show you," she said, then grabbed her notebook and sank down to the concrete floor, cross-legged, and began sketching.

She stopped briefly to pat the floor, and he joined her, watching as her hand raced across the page. She'd sketched out what she'd just described. A rudimentary sketch, but even to his untrained eye, it was damn good.

"What do you think?"

"I think you can draw," he said drily.

She rolled her eyes. "Thanks."

"But seriously. You're really good, and I also think that's a great idea."

"Cool. I just really want it to have that sexy look that women love, but also a very natural feel. Not just a posed beefcake style of shot. But something that feels more real."

He nodded. "I'm good with that."

She closed the sketchbook, and they discussed locations, plans, and dates for each guy for the next few weeks. When they were done, he asked her the question he most wanted to know.

"Why do you like to draw so much? Besides that you're talented."

"I've always done it," she said, looking him in the eyes, her voice patently honest. "Ever since I was younger. Since my dad died. I think drawing helped me deal."

Her directness floored him. He wasn't used to that kind of openness. He didn't talk that openly about loss. He didn't even know how. So he did his best to respond in a way that was worthy. "Sort of like therapy?"

"Absolutely," she said. "I was sad so much of the time,

and drawing animals cheered me up."

"Animals with jaunty hats?"

She bumped her shoulder against his, smiling. "In many cases, yes." She pulled up the shirtsleeve, showing him her owl once more. "You asked about a deeper meaning. Here it is: this owl is for my father."

"Can I?" he said, lifting his hand to her shoulder, as if the ink possessed some kind of magical power. Or maybe it was just the chance to touch her once more. He traced his fingertip over the ink, then swallowed thickly. She'd been honest with him; he could do the same for her. Besides, they were keeping a necessary physical distance, so they were safe to talk like this. "I'd love to hear the story."

He heard footsteps on the stairs. One of the guys was on his way down, and that was his cue not to get any closer to Megan. The sound was a reminder of the promise he'd made to Travis.

"But I shouldn't," he added, crossing his arms as if that would distance himself from the pull he felt toward her. He didn't want to be harsh, but being so close to her would only lead to trouble. "We shouldn't," he added in as cold a voice as he could muster.

Her features registered a strange sort of surprise. She seemed taken aback at first, then nodded crisply, as if she understood. But her eyes said otherwise.

He turned away from her. He had to.

Chapter Eight

"I know this is going to be really hard for you, Trav. But try your best to look smoldering."

Travis gave her a pouty glare as he narrowed his eyes. "I'm always smoldering."

"I didn't say I needed you to speak. You just keep your mouth shut and let me shoot," Megan said as she captured a few final images of her shirtless brother standing by the WELCOME TO HIDDEN OAKS sign on the corner of the winding two-lane highway that connected visitors to the town where they both grew up.

She appraised the morning's take on the LCD screen on the back of the camera, pleased with her brother's contribution. She liked that this year's calendar would feature the guys around town, in more natural environments.

"How do they look?"

"If I Photoshop someone else's face on, they'll be great," Megan said in a deadpan voice.

"Oh, ha ha. You know calendar sales would dwindle to nothing without me."

"Enough, enough. Put your shirt on. You're about the only fireman I don't want to see shirtless," Megan said as she tucked her camera into the bag. There was no need for lights, since the natural light of the morning had done its job, bathing the shot in a warm glow. The golden hour, she called this time of day.

"Hey now," Travis said as he pulled on his T-shirt. "I don't want you getting involved with any firemen."

"You don't have to worry about that," Megan said quickly. Too quickly. She changed topics. "Breakfast?"

"Bella's, of course," Travis said, and they walked around the corner about a hundred feet to a restaurant that looked like a miniature red barn on the outside, complete with the red paneling and a tarnished rooster weather vane on the roof. The restaurant was named after the owner's dog, and the sign was written in script with a paw print as the final flourish.

"Morning, Megan. Morning, Travis," said Theresa, the restaurant owner.

"Hey, Theresa," Megan said. "Good to see you."

"Glad you're back in town. Think we might keep you this time?"

"Wish I could, but I've got Portland in my crosshairs," Megan said, because she was ready for her adventure as soon as she finished the calendar. While in town, she was staying at her mom's house, since her mom was on a two-week cruise with her husband. Megan was living out of suitcases. The boxes that Travis had helped her pack up when he came down to Los Angeles last week were stacked in the garage. Untouched. There weren't many. Clothes, pencils, sketchpads, makeup, and photography equipment. All her books were on her ereader, and she owned no furniture. Never had. She didn't like things, except for her drawings, and those stayed with her.

Being back at the house was tough for her—it brought back memories of all those days when her mom didn't even want to get out of bed. Megan had tried valiantly to help her mom cope in the only way she knew how: by drawing her pictures for comfort. Her mom still had a boxful of drawings—every species of bird under the sun was in Megan's repertoire, not to mention pictures of cartoonish dogs in tutus and even a porcupine wearing a top hat. They'd helped some, earning Megan a smile and a few laughs each time she'd presented one to her mom.

Mostly though, Megan had veered in the other direction of her mom when she was younger, by running to the river, heading to the parks, finding new trails in the woods to explore. Ever since then, she'd had wanderlust in her blood, and it had become a deep-rooted part of her soul.

Theresa seated them at their favorite booth by the window that looked out over curving hills.

"Need a menu?" she asked.

"Nope. I'll have toast and English breakfast tea, please."

Travis chuckled at her order.

"What? What's wrong with that?"

"Toast and tea. It's just funny." Then to Theresa, "The usual for me."

She nodded. "Omelet, hash browns, sausage, toast, and coffee."

Megan laughed. "Someday, Travis, you won't be able to

eat like that."

He stretched his arms out wide and patted his flat stomach. "Maybe. But not yet."

"What's the latest news from Hidden Oaks? You said there was a big fire a few weeks ago. How's the family doing?" Megan asked.

"They're doing okay, actually. Staying with friends while their house is being worked on. But they're all good. I told you their pets are fine, too, right? I saved the dog and cat."

"Aww, that's sweet."

"Becker deserves all the credit. He got the kids from the second floor."

Megan froze. She'd had no idea. But then, why would she? "He did?"

"We were both on duty when the call came in. The parents were at a work dinner and just a sitter was there, but she was maybe twelve and had fallen asleep on the couch. Neighbors called 911 when they smelled the smoke."

Megan clasped her hand over her mouth, then released it. "Oh my God. That's so scary."

"Becker went up through all the smoke. Saved those little kids."

Megan felt a stinging in the back of her eyes. "Wow. That's intense."

"Anyway, so once the kids were safe, I went back in and snagged the dog and the cat. They were both hiding out under the kitchen table. Scared little creatures."

"That's amazing. I mean, you just do something amazing. Going into a burning house and not even thinking twice."

"Let me tell you, there's no one I'd rather have getting my back than Becker. That man is a rock. All the more incredible, considering..."

"Considering what?"

Travis brushed off the question. "Nothing," he said crisply.

"Travis, what were you going to say?" she pressed, wanting to know more about Becker, even though he'd tried to push her away at the end of their chat at the firehouse.

"He's just seen some bad shit, okay? And by the way, I already told him to stay away from you."

Her jaw dropped. "What?"

He pointed to his eyes. "I have two eyes. I saw you chatting the other day at the coffee shop. I'd trust him with my life, but he's no good for you, so don't get any ideas."

She willed herself to give nothing away, to not reveal that he had indeed picked up on mutual attraction. "One. Nothing is going to happen. Two. Why on earth would you say that?"

"He's not in a good space. He had a rough go of it in Chicago. He'd never be able to give you what you need. Just trust me on this," Travis said.

"That's just fine," she replied as matter-of-factly as she could, trying to make it seem like there was no reason for him to be concerned anyway. "Besides, I'm not interested in a relationship with anyone right now. I'm not even going to be in town for long," she said, speaking the full truth. There was another side to the truth, though; she already liked Becker and she knew that spending more time with him would lead to her wanting more of a relationship, and that would simply be no good for her heart.

"What's the story, Miss Megan? You really going to Portland?"

"Yes," she said. Now was as good a time as any to tell him about the job she'd landed, so she shared the details. As she finished, she added, "And that means I'm only in town for as long as the shoot and then I'll be on my way again."

Travis's expression turned wistful as he sighed. "I'm happy for you. But I wish you were staying. Not going to lie. I hate that you're leaving again so soon."

"I know you do, but this is a big deal for me."

"I get it. It's just good to have you back. I like having you around. Call me crazy for liking my sister," he said and flashed a half-sad, half-happy smile.

"*Crazy*," she said as if it were a nickname. Then she let go of the teasing. "Thanks for coming to get me in L.A." She was grateful for her big brother. They were a team; always had been, always would be. He'd looked out for her when they were younger, and he was the first person she called when she decided it was finally time to get away from the toxic relationship with Jason. Travis had responded instantly, heading down to L.A. the next day to help her.

"Of course. That guy was a douche. I'm glad he wasn't there when I picked you up or I would have strangled him. You heard from him at all?"

"No. I honestly don't even think he knows I'm gone. Or he doesn't care," Megan said, then felt a hitch in her throat. She hadn't shed many tears over Jason lately. She'd shed them all while they were together for those two long years, and he'd been ghosting in and out of moments in her life, existing on another plane of reality—his own heightened reality. Recalling the emptiness that had been her time with him brought so many latent emotions to the surface. Add in her already-keyed-up response to the story of the fire, and her eyes were wet again.

"Hey," Travis said softly and switched sides to join Megan. He wrapped an arm around his little sister. "It's okay."

She leaned into his shoulder, tucking her face against his navy-blue T-shirt as a few rebel tears fell. "Sorry," she muttered. "It's not even that I miss him. It was just such a crap relationship."

He stroked her hair. "I know. It sounds like it. I'm really glad you're not with him. You deserve a good guy. A stable, steady guy who'd never hurt you and who'd never do that shit."

She wiped away her last remaining tear. "What about you? Anyone in your life?"

"Hell no," Travis said. "You know me. I'm married to my two jobs."

"I know. And I still worry about you every day. The thought of you going into that burning building and something happening to you is horrifying."

He flashed her his cocky grin. "I'm a gambler. I take my chances." Then he turned serious. "But you know me. It's in my blood. Just like Dad."

"And that's what scares me. The same thing happening to you."

"I do everything I can to keep on living. Everything."

"I wish you were just a professional card player." Megan wasn't fond of her brother's volunteer career whatsoever. She'd tried to talk him out of it many times over the years, but he was determined. She'd had to live with the fear, and some days it threatened to eat her alive.

"I've got some new executive card games I'm working. And I've been teaching a few VCs down in San Fran how to play better. How to bluff and whatnot."

"See? Why can't you just do that full time? You're good at it."

"Because I'm a fireman. It's part of who I am. It's all I ever knew. All I ever wanted to do. Dad died trying to save a family. I sure as hell don't want to die, but my goal is to honor him by helping people, too."

"I hate the thought of something happening to you," she said, flinching painfully at the prospect of losing him. She didn't want to linger in this conversation, though. Travis knew how she felt. "Tell me something pleasant. Tell me something nice you remember about Dad."

"Something nice about Dad," Travis said, and his eyes drifted off to the far wall of the restaurant lined with framed illustrations of cows, chickens, and eggs. "He used to read to you when you were little. Every single night. He came home, tucked you in, and made sure he read to you. You always wanted stories of animals. That was your favorite thing in the whole world, and he read them all to you."

Megan wished she could remember it. Wished she knew more of her father than her own inked interpretation and childhood fantasy that he'd watched over her. But she didn't, and she never would.

As far as she was concerned, that was yet another reminder of why it was a damn good thing she and Becker had agreed to keep their hands off each other. Because the more she got to know him, the more she liked him. And the more she liked him, the more likely she'd be hurt. A man like that, driven by danger, could ruin a woman's heart.

Even so, there was a part of her that longed to know him, to see past all the things that Travis warned her about.

To understand that dark and haunted look she'd seen in Becker's eyes. Maybe even to help him through. She'd never been able to help Jason because he hadn't wanted it.

But she simply had to ignore that noise in her head.

More than that, she needed to turn the volume all the way down on that little voice—that naughty, devilish voice—that was asking for a repeat of that first night. Just the memory of how Becker had touched her brought a flush to her cheeks and a hot shiver across her skin.

Like a glass of lemonade on a hot day, another night with him might quench her thirst. A night of letting go, giving in, *feeling* everything. But that was crazy to contemplate. Besides, Becker probably wasn't even thinking about her, and as long as they both kept their encounter in its proper place—a cordoned-off, sealed-up box on the far back shelf of a closet—then there would be no problem getting through a little thing like a photo shoot.

No problem whatsoever.

Chapter Nine

When Megan stopped by the Panting Dog the next night to hang out with Jamie, Becker muttered a gruff hello, not even meeting her eyes. It was barely an acknowledgment, and it irked Megan. Rationally, she knew this was for the best. Logically, she understood the need for the distance between them, especially given her conversation with Travis.

Still, it bugged her, so she did her best to divert her attention. She chatted with Jamie, catching up with her good friend and focusing hard on heeding her brother's warning.

"Tell me everything I missed in the last year or so. Well, besides you and Smith," Megan added with a wink.

Jamie brought Megan up to date with various Hidden Oaks locals, from the woman who ran the olive oil shop who'd self-published a naughty romance novel that sold well and had made many husbands happy when their wives read it, to her sister Diane's burgeoning relationship with a kind and caring dentist a few towns over.

"He's the best. He treats Diane so well and she's incredibly happy." Then Jamie's eyes widened and she dropped her voice. "But did your mom ever tell you what happened to Craig?" she asked, concern in her voice, as she mentioned the guy who managed Megan's mom's bookstore.

"She said he was on crutches from a ski accident, but I never got all the details. What happened?"

"He was training for an MS fund-raiser up at Squaw in the winter. A kid on a snowboard swooped in front of him, he swerved out of the way, and bam," Jamie said, as she smacked her hands together to approximate a loud, crashing sound.

Megan cringed. "Oh my God. No," she said, as if she could stop the pain that was surely part of this story.

"He was in a coma for three days from the fall. But wait—it has a happy ending. He pulled through. He woke up to find his leg broken in several spots. I mean, he had a hell of a run of bad luck, but he went back to work in a cast and crutches a few weeks ago."

Megan breathed a sigh of relief. "Thank God. That's so scary, but I'm so glad it all worked out. All things considered," she said. "My mom said he was back at work quickly. Sounds like a real trouper."

They chatted more as Jamie poured Megan a beer, and maybe it was the memory of the first Chihuahua she had here the other night, or maybe it was just his nearness, but she found her mind drifting back to Becker and her eyes straying to where he sat. A ribbon of longing unfurled in her as she flashed back on the way they talked by the truck the other morning before he turned away, then to how they slipped easily into conversation that first night. And now, to the way he looked so intense and serious as he seemed to be studying his laptop like it held the keys to the universe, his strong forearms on display in his shirt as he typed.

Those arms...how she wanted to feel them around her again.

Stupid fucking hormones. She loved them and hated them. But she also knew those bastards were powerful, and as she downed her beer, she couldn't deny the rush of heat in her body anymore. This was a safe zone though; they were at the bar, Jamie was here, Smith was on his way, so she saw no reason why she couldn't at least flirt with temptation.

• • •

God, it was killing him to have her nearby. His muscles tensed and his fingers twitched, eager to touch her.

He refused to move, to stand, to walk over to her and dust his lips across that absolutely enticing neck, or wrap his arms around her slim waist and tug her close. Nope. He was holding out, so he'd parked himself in his usual spot at the table by the window after they closed for the night, laptop in front of him, reviewing the operations and emailing suppliers about outstanding orders and new inventory.

But even though she was all the way on the other side of the bar, he had been painfully aware of how close she was as she'd chatted with Jamie for the last half hour. He was a master of restraint, but this would be taxing to any man.

Thankfully, there was a knock on the window. Becker turned to see that Smith had pressed his face against the glass, smushing his mouth and nose against the pane. Becker managed a laugh, rose, and walked to the door and unlocked it.

Smith patted him on the back once. "How's business tonight?"

"Excellent."

"Got your nose in the books, I see? All work and no play…" Smith said, and trailed off his admonishment. Smith was a hard worker, ran his own contracting business, and had recently built out the expanded back section of the bar. But he also was probably a helluva lot better than Becker at letting go of the day and putting work behind him.

"Nice ass."

Smith turned to the bar where Jamie was wiping down the counter and catcalling her boyfriend.

"Why, thank you, ma'am. I do believe you are its number one fan," Smith said as he turned and patted his backside.

Megan swiveled around, joining Jamie in the hooting and hollering. For the briefest of moments, he envied her ease, her free spirit. Out of the corner of his eye, he lingered on the group, wanting to tear his gaze away from her but completely unable to. She caught his stare and flashed a grin in his direction. Lingered, too, her eyes locked on him, like she didn't want to look away. Hell, he didn't want to, either. He wanted everyone to leave, to pull down the blinds, lock the door, and lift her up on the bar and kiss the hell out of her. Feel her melt into his arms again.

He wanted that so much that it nearly pained him to look away.

"You gonna join us for a drink?" Smith asked him.

"I need to finish up this inventory analysis," he said, staring at the computer screen.

"Then you definitely need a drink, even if it's only a Shirley Temple."

"I'll catch you later, man," Becker said. If he closed his laptop and joined them at the bar, he didn't know that he'd be able to keep his hands off Megan. If he were in the same five-foot vicinity, he didn't think he'd be able to resist running a thumb over her hip bone, watching the look in her eyes shift from playful to hungry as her lips parted and her breathing intensified. He wouldn't say a word, he'd just grab her hand, pull her into the supply closet, and have an encore of the other night.

Numbers became his best friend now, and for the next several minutes he ran report after report on suppliers, on inventory, on the bar's monthly sales until that was all that was in his head.

"Working hard?"

So much for his concentration. There she was, sliding into the seat across from him, fixing that sexy grin on him.

"Trying my best," he said.

"You run a nice bar," she said, waving her hand around to show the inside of the Panting Dog. "I was thinking about it when I was out for a hike this morning."

"Glad you like it. Glad it kept you occupied on the trails."

"It did and I do. I'm tempted to have another Chihuahua," she said, lowering her voice as she mentioned the beer she'd had with him that first night.

"Yeah? You liked that Chihuahua?" He lifted an eyebrow, cautious about engaging in this sort of banter, but eager, too.

"I did. I liked it a lot," she said, her mouth forming a gorgeous O on the last word.

He shut his eyes briefly, letting the quick bolt of lust roll through him. Then he opened them. "You're making it hard to work," he said, lowering his voice.

"Am I? Making it hard?"

He swallowed. His throat was dry. "Yes," he said, his skin heating up. She glanced briefly at the bar. Smith and Jamie were laughing at something as they walked to the back section, leaving them alone.

"Megan," he whispered as a warning.

"Yes?" she said, dropping her hand below the table and tap-dancing her fingers along his knee.

He drew a deep, fueling breath. "What are you doing to me?"

The expression on her face shifted from the flirty-playful look to a more serious one. "I don't know," she admitted. "I'm supposed to be staying away from you."

"Yeah, and vice versa."

"My brother even told me to."

"Did he?"

"Yep. He said he thought we were checking each other out at coffee the other day."

He chuffed a humorless laugh. Travis was too fucking observant for his own good. Or maybe Becker was just too obvious. "Were we? Checking each other out?"

"Well, considering that was after you sent me all those naughty text messages, I would definitely have to say so," she said, wiggling an eyebrow.

Now he laughed for real. "All those naughty text messages? If memory serves, there were only a few even sent."

She shrugged happily. "Maybe then I was just thinking of all the other ones I wanted to send."

Desire slammed into him once more, like a punishing wave. He had to stay very, very still, or else he'd have no choice but to get that woman naked and up against the wall.

"Were you now?"

"I was."

"Like what?"

She kept her gaze locked on him, never wavering, as she dropped her voice to a heated whisper. "Like how I wanted you again. All the different ways."

"What sort of ways?" he asked, playing with fire, but doing it anyway.

She glanced around, maybe needing her own confirmation that the coast was clear, then leaned closer, her breasts brushing the table, her gorgeous face near enough for him to kiss. "Right now I'm thinking about how much I'd like to be on top of you on that chair."

He hissed in a breath. His eyes grew hazy; his sanity seemed to have slunk away. Restraint was walking on a path out the door.

"I like the way you look on top of me," he said, low and hot.

"I like the way I feel when I'm on top of you."

"How do I make you feel?" he asked, going on a hunting expedition. But hell, she was a willing partner, and he told himself they were safe enough right here. This was all talk, no action, so it was fine.

"Like there's nothing else in the world. Like you want nothing more than to make me feel amazing," she said, her voice feathery.

"That's what I wanted the night we were together. I loved making you feel good. The fact that I only made you come twice pissed me off," he said, keeping his hands on the table and out of trouble.

She breathed out the sexiest little sigh. One only he could hear. Meant only for him. Full of need and desire. "But you've made me come more than twice," she said, keeping her eyes hooked on him as she confessed.

He tried to suppress a grin. He tried to fight off the images dominating his brain, but it was near impossible when all he could see was her alone, legs spread, fingers flying, moans piercing the silence. "How did I do it? The time I wasn't there."

She parted her lips to answer, and he was dying to know what she'd pictured, when a loud voice called out.

"We're thinking of doing a little midnight bowling. Who's going to join? It's on me since I won the pancake bet and served the most flapjacks at the fund-raiser."

Smith had returned with his arm draped around Jamie, and Becker wanted to strangle his friend and thank him at the same time. Because he was picturing the scene that would have unfolded next. She'd grab at his hair in a frenzied rush, and he'd yank off her shirt, and there'd be little time for anything more than the main attraction. He'd spin her around, hike up that crazy short skirt she was wearing, pull down her panties, and she'd be ready. Hot and wet and inviting. He'd run a hand down the soft, smooth skin of her back, watching as her spine bowed in a ridiculously sexy way that made him harder than he'd ever been, and then she'd say, *Now. Take me now.*

Yeah, Becker decided he'd send a thank-you note to Smith. Because there was no way he'd have stopped otherwise.

"You three go. I need to finish up," he said.

Megan rose, shot him a brief look that was both lusty

and wistful, then left.

He was rock-hard, and he was still turned on thirty minutes later when he unlocked the door to his dark and quiet home. But he wasn't going to give in. He went to bed, keeping his hands to himself, as if that would keep the thoughts of her at bay.

Becker's dreams were restless that night, as they were every night. They were bits and pieces—stuck in a building he couldn't find his way out of, endless stairwells that rose and fell in all directions, paths in the woods that went nowhere and everywhere at the same time. He was used to these demons by now, too familiar with the way nighttime ushered in agitation in his mind.

He wished he was dreaming of something pleasant, maybe a quiet run in the woods, or a barbecue, even a walk with a dog.

A light flashed from his nightstand and he reached for his phone. There was a text from Megan.

Didn't want to leave you hanging. But it was reverse cowgirl, and it was toe-curlingly good. Good night.

Well, there went any and all resistance.

He latched onto the image instantly, and he instructed his brain to stay there the rest of the night, to never stray from her legs, and belly, and long neck that invited kisses. It was far more pleasant than his previous dreams.

Though "pleasant" wasn't entirely the right word. More like "too hot to let go of."

Pictures raced across his closed eyelids. The swell of her breasts. The curve of her waist. The smooth skin of her belly.

Ah, hell. Sometimes the brain needed a helping hand. He pushed off the sheets, took his hard length in his hand, and imagined Megan.

Straddling him.

Lowering herself onto him.

Moaning as she took him in.

He'd grab her hips and bring her down on him hard, filling her completely. He pictured how she'd look riding him right now, her long hair flowing down her back, taking him reverse-cowgirl style, rocking up and down on his cock, her glorious wetness nice and snug, as she braced herself on his thighs with her hands. Back bowed, hair falling, just the sides of those gorgeous full breasts visible from his vantage point. He gripped himself harder, stroking faster, picturing Megan on him, making her throaty moans and whimpers.

Slamming in and out of her, until she cried out his name, the sounds of her pleasure sending him over the edge. He jacked himself harder, feeling the build start in the base of his spine. God, it felt good, picturing her, imagining her doing this to him.

Megan, so hot and so beautiful. Megan, a live wire under his touch. Megan, the woman he wanted to fuck, and to lick, and to kiss.

He groaned, her name a long rumble from his throat as he came.

Chapter Ten

Megan parked her bike in the small dirt lot at the base of one of the hiking trails in Hidden Oaks. The single-track trail was rarely used, since it was too bumpy for all but the most resilient of mountain bikers, and it kept away the day hikers, too.

A long, winding path full of switchbacks awaited her, and she could use a good run to plan the rest of the shoot. Running was the perfect backdrop to review her photo plans. After her brother, Smith had been next in front of the camera. Megan had posed him in a traditional sort of shot—leaning against the fire truck, shirtless, staring off in the distance. He was Jamie's man, and Megan had no interest in him, but the subject matter sure made for a fun shoot. One of her favorite photographic assignments, it turned out.

Back in Los Angeles, she'd landed a few quick gigs shooting head shots for aspiring actors, and while she'd wished them all well in their careers, most of them were far too tightly wound to make the shoot fun. But a fireman posing for a calendar? These men had a good time in front of the camera and rolled with it.

Of course, they all made it seem like they were taking one for the team and only tearing off their shirts and flexing their muscles for the good cause behind it. While that was true, Megan knew better. The chance to be ogled was something most of them enjoyed.

As for Becker, she had a hunch he wasn't the preening type. More of the keep-to-himself type. She wanted to find the ideal location for him.

As she hit the trails in the morning fog, she logged not only miles, but a list of locales. There was the requisite vineyard shot with rolling hills and row upon row of grapes. She'd love a shot, too, of one of the men framed against the wide-open curling roads that wound their way around the county. She lingered on that image for a mile or so, cycling through the most picturesque roads nearby.

Then there was the river that looped around the outskirts of Hidden Oaks and lazily drifted down through the other towns. She wasn't far from the river, and the ribbon cut a peaceful image, but a steady one, too. Rocks, water, and a fireman, maybe? She rounded a switchback, heading higher uphill on the trail. She hadn't yet passed another runner, but that was often the case this early in the morning. These trails attracted only the stalwarts.

She heard quick footfalls from above. Around the corner came the powerful form of the man she'd slept with. The man she wanted to touch again, but couldn't and shouldn't. The man she'd sent that naughty text to last night.

Megan should have been surprised to see him, but she

wasn't. Because it made all the sense in the world that he came here in the early hours of the dawn, too. He might as well have been carved from solitude. His head was down, and he wore a dark T-shirt that revealed his stunning arms, and running shorts that showed off strong legs. A slight sheen of sweat glistened on his forehead. He saw her and slowed to a jog.

"Good morning, Miss Tattoo Artist."

"Good morning, Mr. Bar Owner," she returned with a wink.

"How was bowling last night?"

"Great. I won a round, Smith won a round, and Jamie landed a strike. How was your night?"

"Restless for a bit. But then my mind wandered to something 'toe-curlingly good,'" he said, sketching air quotes around her words.

She tried to rein in a flirty smile but had no luck. "Wish I'd been there to help."

"If you were with me, there wouldn't be any helping going on."

She arched an eyebrow. "Well, aren't you Mr. Independent?"

He leaned forward, dipped his head to her neck, and said in a husky voice in her ear, "If you were with me, I'd be so deep inside you that you'd barely be able to form words."

"What would I be able to do?" she asked, her voice feather-thin.

"You'd have your legs wrapped tight around me and you'd only be able to moan and scream in pleasure," he said, his lips dangerously close to her skin, so close she was dying for him to lick her, kiss her, touch her. "And incidentally, I love those sounds that you make."

She swayed as desire flooded all the corners of her body, goose bumps rising across every inch. Her skin felt electric. Her brain was firing images at her like a movie reel in fast-forward. Flesh against hot flesh. Fingers exploring everywhere. "That's not fair," she finally managed to say as he backed away.

"I know," he said, his lips curving up. "Nor was your text last night."

There was a tight line of tension between them. They were all alone in the world, wrapped in only the mist of the early-morning fog. Fog doesn't tell secrets. Fog shields stolen kisses. They could veer off this path and find a spot on the grass, or a tree, and he could take her standing up, as she held on for dear life. They could get tangled up in the woods, surrounded only by the chirping of birds and the quiet murmurs of the river gurgling down below.

She briefly flashed back to the conversation with her brother, to his warnings. But he wasn't here now, and she didn't want to think about him. She didn't want to worry or fret over what Travis would think if she spent more time with Becker. He'd already made it clear he didn't want her to. Right now, though, she abolished those thoughts. Because, fuck it. She wanted to think about this man, to touch this man, to talk to this man. She wanted to know more about him, about the things he'd seen, about why Travis had warned her off. And though she had no intention of getting serious with a fireman, her intentions were not on a relationship at the moment—they were on exactly what she'd wanted from him in the first place. A little bit more.

Rather than jump him right now like her body was

begging her to—a damn cheering squad inside her chest was urging her to just do that—she chose a parallel path to her goal.

"I'm running to the river. I was thinking you might look good there for your photo shoot."

He raised his eyebrows playfully, and the expression on his face led to a fluttering in her chest. He was so intense, but then there was that tease, that taunt, as if he wanted to reel her in. Becker had tall, dark, and brooding down pat, but then he chased it with a touch of smart-ass and a full dose of kindness. A potent combination she could get addicted to if she didn't watch out. "You were thinking about me while you were running?"

"Yes. I was," she said. "What do you think about when you're running?"

"I run not to think."

Of course. Of course he does. "Do you want to run the rest of the way with me or not?"

"I don't know that I could keep up with you," he said, and Megan was surprised. She'd expected him to say the obvious guy thing— *I don't know if you can keep up with me.* But he'd turned it around into something of a compliment.

"Why don't we see?"

She took off, leading the way up the final switchback, then maintaining a steady speed down the other side of the hill. Running faster than usual, but not so much that she'd overdo it, she could see the river coming into closer view, and she was sure she'd be the first to the finish line. Her heart was pounding, her lungs were firing on all cylinders, and her calves were working overtime, but surely she could do it.

In one swift motion, like the horse you didn't see coming

on the final turn, Becker flew past her, all six foot and then some of strong, broad, and muscled frame, beating her soundly as he tapped a big hand on the rock that marked the edge of the river.

She finished a few seconds behind him, collapsing onto the rock and laughing.

"Something funny?"

But he was laughing, too. She wasn't even sure why either of them found this so amusing. Maybe it was the incredulity of bumping into him, or maybe it was that they'd gone from bedtime companions, to photographer and subject, to temporary running partners. They could segue easily, it seemed, almost too easily, into these different roles.

"Kind of random to run into you here," she said.

"Is it though? Or did you happen to mention you ran by the river in the mornings?"

Tingles spread across her chest. "Did you come here looking for me?"

He shrugged playfully. "Let's just say I'm not disappointed to have run into you."

"It's almost as if I dropped a hint in the hope that you might pick up on it." she said, taking a step closer to him, wanting to close the distance even more.

"Is that so? You're a fine hint-dropper then, Megan, and I hope you don't mind bumping into me."

She shook her head. "I don't mind it at all. Even though you beat me in our race. And you were letting me think the whole time that I might beat you, weren't you?"

He nodded proudly. "That was my MO."

"You are sneaky." She smacked him on the chest. His very hard, very firm chest.

"Now you're playing dirty. I can't smack you on your chest."

"I'm sure you could find ways to play dirty," she said, and he tilted his head, watching her, waiting for her to make the next move even though they'd agreed on no moves. "But we're not going to do that."

He shook his head. "We're not going to do that at all," he said, as he looked down at her hand still on his chest. A spark shot through her and desire took over. She spread her palm open against his T-shirt.

A low rumble emanated from his throat. She quirked up the corner of her lips, her fingertips now dancing across his chest. Her hands had a mind of their own, as his chest became a playground. Her index finger traced the outline of his pecs, then darted down to those abs, sharply defined even through the T-shirt, like a ladder from his chest down to that terribly tempting waistband of his running shorts.

That was the problem. He was so tantalizing to her. He was all man, all raw speed and strength. He could sling her over his shoulder and carry her for miles without breaking a sweat. Not that she wanted or needed to be carried, yet she found herself craving—intensely craving, deep in her gut—the shape of him, the size of him, the way he could overpower her in seconds.

That combination of sheer power and utter control ratcheted up her hunger for him. She splayed her fingers across his abdomen, her pinkie inching close to his shorts, imagining what lay beneath. She wanted to feel him, to wrap her hand around him again, to take him all the way into her mouth.

"Now you are playing dirty," he said, his voice a hoarse whisper. "And if you go any farther, I'm not going to want to stop."

"Me neither," she whispered, then hung her head. Reluctantly, she moved her hand away, and the lack of contact felt like a sharp pain. Like a void that needed to be filled, but couldn't because there were lines you cross and lines you don't cross. She loved her brother more than anyone, and she didn't want to disappoint him. Nor did she want to disappoint herself. Even though they weren't on a path to a real future, she could already feel the first tugs of something with Becker, something more than the fling she'd envisioned the morning after they met. She pictured it playing out if they spent more time together, and she could sense how easily she could slide from wanting him to wanting *all* of him. Even if they returned to Plan A and simply enjoyed each other's company while she was in town, she was sure she'd fall hard for him.

With no safety net in sight.

She'd vowed never to fall for a man with a dangerous job, because she had the blueprint of what she might become. She'd seen it in her own mother for years. A vacuum. A black hole of years missed.

Images flickered by. A photo album of lost days and nights, with pictures of her mother leaving Megan and Travis to get themselves up every morning, make breakfast, pack lunch boxes, then find their own way home after school. They'd come home, make the dinner, do the laundry, help each other with homework, lean on each other more than her.

Slowly, steadily her mom climbed her way out of the grief and the sorrow, and Megan found it hard to fault her for that kind of reaction to the love of your life dying. But she certainly didn't want to chance that kind of life herself, no matter how much heat flared between her and Becker.

She stared off at the river, slow-moving and meandering, moseying on down the riverbed, crossing rocks that jutted out of the mud. "I used to spend so much time here when I was a kid. I always ran off to the river when I was sad," she said as she sank down on a rock. Maybe it was the river, maybe it was the memories, maybe it was him asking a simple *yeah?* that led her to keep talking as he joined her. "And then sometimes when I wasn't sad. It just became my place, like a safe spot where I couldn't get hurt. Travis started coming with me and we'd hang out by the river. I felt like this was the only place in the whole wide world that was immune to trouble."

"What'd you guys do here?"

"We made mud pies. The best mud pies in the whole county. One time, we loaded them up in the crate attached to the back of my bike, and brought them back into town. We set up a little stand with a card table in the town square and tried to sell our mud pies."

He laughed softly. "Get any takers?"

"Shockingly, no. But the local paper took our picture so we thought we were hot shit. Then we decided to bake brownies and sell those instead, and let me tell you—thanks to our mud pie picture in the paper we made a killing with our brownie stand. Called them Mud Pie Brownies."

"And no one was worried they were actually made with mud?"

She gave him a sideways glance. "I was eight. Travis was twelve. We knew everyone. We weren't trying to hoodwink the people of Hidden Oaks. But we did include extra dark chocolate and that's why everyone loved them so much."

"You still make Mud Pie Brownies?"

"Sometimes. I'm not that into cooking, but I'm damn good at baking."

"What else?"

"What else do I bake?"

He smiled lightly, then shook his head. "What else did you do at the river?"

His voice had a soft quality to it, or maybe he was just relaxed, sitting here on a rock with her, enjoying her stories of how she'd grown up.

"I can make an excellent dam. Don't make a beaver joke," she added quickly, fixing him with a serious stare.

He held up his hands in surrender. "No beaver jokes, I swear."

"It's all because of Travis. He taught me. We could spend hours laying twigs and stones and branches right over there." She pointed to a bend in the river. "Doing everything we could to divert a little bit of water, and to see how long the dam would hold. He said it was, and I quote"—she began imitating her brother's voice—"a vital skill for any sister of mine to have."

Becker nodded. "I can hear him saying that. It sounds like him."

Maybe talking about her brother wasn't such a good idea, since he didn't want anything to happen between them. Even so, she had such fond memories of her times with Travis here at the river, and sharing those stories with Becker simply felt right. This river was her place, the spot she'd run to, the place where she felt at peace with the world and all the terrible things that had happened to her family. The place she'd been when she decided to get her owl.

She glanced over her shoulder at her owl. At its permanence on her skin. "The owl you asked about?"

"Yes." His eyes never strayed from her.

"When I was younger, maybe seven or eight, there was an owl who showed up outside my house every night for several weeks. I swear this owl stood like a sentry by the peaked roof over the garage. I could see him from my second-floor bedroom window, and the owl seemed as if he was watching me with those unblinking eyes."

"Owls do that, don't they?"

His voice was calm and strong, and though she'd rarely shared her story before, she felt comfortable telling him. "I used to pretend the owl was an emissary for my father, guarding me, keeping me safe, watching over me. I'd grab my notebook and colored pencils, fling open the window, and stand at the windowsill to draw the creature," she said, and she could hear the wistfulness in her own voice as she told the story that was so crystal clear in her memory. "And that's why I have an owl on my shoulder."

"For your father," he said, with something like reverence in his voice.

"To keep him close to me. To remember him."

"That's beautiful. Reminds me of soldiers who lose men on the battlefield and remember their fallen brothers with a tattoo," he said, his dark eyes intensely serious.

"Or cops. Or firefighters," she offered, and he looked away briefly, and winced as if the mention was too much.

She laid a gentle hand on his arm, and he turned his gaze back to her.

"Thank you for sharing that story," he said softly. "I'd

have thought it was a symbol of wisdom or something. But this just shows that even symbols are personal."

"They are," she said, and she was tempted to run her fingertips along his jawline, or gently finger a strand of the soft, thick hair that she'd loved holding on to the other night.

"And is that one of the reasons why you want to open your own tattoo shop in Portland someday?"

A grin broke across her face. "I never told you I wanted to open a shop," she said, but she wasn't annoyed. She was impressed that he'd figured it out.

"I know," he said, raising his eyebrows in playful acknowledgment. "But I put two and two together and figured that was your long-term goal with the job you're taking."

"Yeah, that's what I want to do. Don't get me wrong—I like photography. But I think I could be happy for a long, long time doing tattoos. I love drawing, and I like that tattoos matter to the people who are getting them. I spent a week in San Diego last year, learning from this guy Trey who works at a shop there, and has all this beautiful art on his body for his family, and for his young daughter and his wife. It's gorgeous work, and she has some designs on her body too. It's this deep and meaningful expression of love and hope," she said, and a part of her expected him to shut down from all this openness, all this talking. He was a man who'd admitted he liked barriers. But he didn't start layering bricks around himself. He listened. He understood. She kept going. Being here made her feel adventurous, and she was eager to know more about this man. "What about you? How did you know you wanted to be a fireman?" she asked, tilting her head and looking at his beautiful face and his haunting brown eyes.

He leaned forward, resting his hands on his thighs and

meeting Megan's inquisitive stare. "When I was nine I was out riding bikes with my brother. Griffin's two years younger than me, but a sturdy kid who knew how to ride. Even so, he fell off his bike while turning onto a nearby street too sharply. Knocked into the curb and crashed. Broke his arm. A piece of the bone was sticking out," Becker said, as he recounted.

Megan winced at the image.

"I ditched my bike on the sidewalk, picked him up, and carried him all the way home while he cried, making sure the arm didn't move," he continued. "My mom wasn't home, so I found a scarf, turned it into a sling, and tied it at his neck, even though I'd never done it before." He mimed the motions as he told the story. "Then I called her; she raced home and took him to the hospital to get it set."

"Wow," Megan said, in awe. "It's like you knew what to do on an instinctual, innate level. You knew how to make a sling, keep a bone immobile."

"Yeah, I think it just kind of fit. It was just something that I could do. So, honestly, this is what I've always known. Always done."

Megan felt a warmth in her chest that had nothing to do with desire and everything to do with admiration. His job was dangerous, but it was beautiful too, and the way he told the story made her see it ever so briefly in a different light. Maybe it was because he was a lover—a onetime lover— rather than a part of her family. That gave her enough distance for now to see the job through the prism of something other than her usual worry and fear.

"I love that story." He was calmness, he was patience, he was the person holding your hand while cutting you out of a car toppled over on the side of the road. "It's like you were graced with the natural instinct to save."

Something dark passed over his eyes, and he clenched his fists as he looked away. "Don't say that," he muttered. "Don't say stuff like that."

"Why?" she asked softly.

He shook his head and didn't answer her. Just scrubbed a hand across his stubbled jaw and exhaled hard.

"Hey," she said, softly placing a hand on his shoulder. He tensed but didn't flinch. "You okay?"

He nodded.

She wanted to ask why he'd moved to Hidden Oaks, what he'd left behind in Chicago. She wanted to tell him she was amazed at how he'd rescued those kids a few weeks ago. Yet she knew none of those things were what he needed to hear right now. That now wasn't the time for praise or for inquisition.

"Where's your brother now? Is he still in Chicago?"

He shook his head. "Nope. He's in L.A. Where you used to be."

She raised her eyebrows in curiosity. "Is he an actor? Screenwriter? Director? Model?" she asked, rattling off the most common professions.

He laughed. "He's an animator at a visual effects house. He does some amazing design work, and he emails a lot of it to me in advance, so I'm pretty lucky getting to see his work before anyone else. He's the *sensitive, artistic* one," he added playfully.

"Don't kid yourself. You're sensitive, too."

He pretended to cringe.

"You are," she said insistently. "And I like it. Anyway, so

you're a fireman and he's an animator," she said, stretching her arms out wide to show the distance between the two jobs.

"Don't forget bar owner," he added. "Though I believe I could say the same for you. Your brother's a fireman and you're a photographer who loves to draw, and would rather be inking designs on people's skin."

A smile bloomed on her face. He understood her so well already. "Yes, that's me. And that's so cool that your brother's an artist too. I'd love to see some of the movies he's worked on."

"You'd like his stuff. He worked on an animated flick most recently, and was responsible for making sure the feathers on a talking bird looked realistic."

"Speaking of animals, the talking and non-talking variety, I'm working on your raccoon," she offered in a light voice as she stood. He rose with her. She watched his profile, and the corner of his lips quirked up.

"Are you now?"

She nodded. "Yep. Someday you're going to have a raccoon tattoo. I just know it."

"From your mouth to…" he trailed off as he turned to look at her, his eyes hooked on her mouth as he said those words. He reached toward her, running a finger across her lips. "Your beautiful, gorgeous mouth."

Time stopped for a moment as she took in his words, his gesture, and the thoroughly tender and completely seductive way he talked to her. The seconds started again when he leaned forward, lightly dusting her lips with his. Then he broke the kiss and rested his forehead against hers. "Megan," he said, his voice rough and full of need. "You make it so hard to resist you. I'm trying, I swear I'm trying. But I don't know how to right now."

She ached all over for him, a sweet and agonizing ache, and all she wanted was to soothe it. "I don't know how to, either."

Like falling snow that melts when it hits the ground, her reasons turned into nothing. Because this—the connection between them—this was something.

She also didn't want to resist him. So she kissed him back. She didn't take her time. She didn't move in slowly. Instead, she gripped his hair in her fingers and kissed him deep and hard.

• • •

He wouldn't be getting any awards for self-control. He wouldn't be receiving a plaque for honoring a buddy's wish.

At the moment, he didn't have it in him to care.

When her lips fused with his as if nothing else mattered in the world, he lost all sense of why he wasn't supposed to touch her. He forgot Travis's warning in the press of her body, in the taste of her breath, in the sweet smell of her hair.

She was leading the kiss; her lips were crushing his, and she'd gone from curious and inquisitive to fevered and bursting with need. He liked both parts of her, maybe more than he should. He liked that she was open and caring, that she was fiery in the bedroom, and he liked the free spirit he saw in her. Right now though, what he liked most of all was how her touch made his body buzz, like his bones were humming. His mind went hazy, his dark thoughts slunk away, and all he was left with was the pure rush of the physical—the bolt of heat that tore through him, her sexy whimpers as they devoured each other in a frenzy of teeth and lips and tongue, her fingers speared through his hair, holding on for dear life, it seemed.

Pleasure forked in his body, rippling through his veins, and he was reduced to nothing more than *want*. He spun her around, backed her up against a nearby tree, and tugged up her T-shirt. "I need to touch you," he rasped in her ear.

She moaned as he spread his fingers across the soft flesh of her belly. Shivering under his touch, her back bowed and her hips jutted out.

It was an invitation, one he was damn sure he had no choice but to RSVP to. He ran his fingertips along her skin, tracing her belly button, her hips, the edge of the waistband of her shorts. He dipped his head to her neck and licked a path up her neck, her skin so hot. "I want you so much. More than I should. More than I'm supposed to. But I just don't care because right now I want to hear the sweet, sexy sounds you make when I touch you," he said, his voice gravelly.

"I can't stop, either. So don't you dare," she said. She grappled at his shirt, her hands frantic as she pulled and tugged at his clothes, as if she couldn't get him near enough. He felt her fingers grasping at his shorts, jerking him even closer.

He groaned as he pressed against her, his cock hard and heavy, and he wished he had a condom with him, so he could strip off her clothes, pull down his shorts, and thrust into her. He slid his hand between her legs, feeling the heat of her desire through her shorts. She gasped the second he made contact; she was so ready to have him inside her.

She moaned again, and it started as a long, low sigh that

became his name. *"Becker."*

"Do you have any idea how much I want to be inside you?"

She nodded against him. "As much as I want you there," she answered quickly, her voice ragged.

"I want to bury myself inside you right now. I want to feel you gripping me," he whispered huskily against her neck.

"And then?" she asked, rocking against his hand, greedily seeking out his fingers even through the layers between them.

"You'll give yourself to me, spread your legs wide open, take me all the way in."

"I will," she said, as she shuddered in his arms. He wrapped a hand around her waist, keeping her steady.

"Then I'll kiss you while I fuck you," he whispered into her ear.

She gasped, and wriggled her body closer to his. "I want that. All of it. I want fucking and kissing," she said, her breathing turning more erratic.

"I'll fuck you like I kiss you, and kiss you like I fuck you. With nothing held back," he said, his tongue darting against the salty skin of her neck as she trembled against him.

"Do that to me now," she said, her breathing turning erratic, her sounds reminding him how close they were flirting with danger.

Too close.

Like the moment before a back draft.

"We shouldn't be doing this," he muttered, but words like that were pointless when she turned the tables, slipping an agile hand inside his shorts, and with a quickness he hadn't expected, wrapping those fingers around his cock.

"I know," she said as she caressed him. "We shouldn't be doing this at all."

She felt so fucking fantastic that he was damn near ready to throw all caution to the wind and fuck her without a glove, but there was no way that would happen. Hell, if she kept stroking him with those soft, talented fingers, he was going to come in her hand, and that wasn't acceptable either. With all the self-restraint he possessed, he removed her hand from his briefs.

"If I stop now, I won't feel like a total ass," he said through gritted teeth.

She nodded, her eyes wild and hazy. She pushed a hand through her hair. "Stop. Yes. No assholes allowed here," she said, as if she were reminding herself.

Somehow, they managed to untangle themselves from each other, to readjust their clothes, to breathe normally again, and they started to walk to the dirt parking lot not too far away. She stopped briefly, pointing to the meandering river, the only witness to their entanglement moments ago. "Hey, Becker. I really do think we should shoot you by the river."

"Yeah? Why's that?"

"Because you look good by the water. It suits you."

It was a shoot. It was only a photo shoot. He'd managed restraint that should earn him a goddamn Olympic gold medal. He could do that again. He took a beat, nodded once, and never stopped looking at her, her beautiful brown eyes captivating him. "Then we'll shoot by the river."

"How about tomorrow morning?"

"Same time?"

"Morning light is the best light," she said as they resumed

their path.

He didn't say out loud that there'd be nobody there in the morning. Just like today. He didn't want to acknowledge the temptation. Maybe because he wanted to believe he could manage it. He wanted to believe nothing could harm his friendship with Travis.

• • •

Her hand was itching to touch his. The desire to be connected to him physically was like electricity, stirring the air. Given how he'd touched her only moments ago, her body was still vibrating with need. She craved the feel of his strong hand in hers, and the force of that desire surprised her.

Yet it felt entirely natural to want that from Becker.

As they walked to the lot together, she lifted her fingers a few times, reaching toward him, then dropping them back down to her side, trapped by this strange indecision. She wanted to stroll to their vehicles together, fingers clasped. That warm, comforting image was so potent right now, and it felt like the right gesture after their morning together. Surely he was the kind of man who'd hold her hand, especially after that near-O she'd just about achieved.

But then, there was something about holding hands that felt like a promise of more. More times, more moments, more connection. Almost-orgasms were one thing; deeper intimacy was another. Holding hands while walking together would be another line to cross. It was the quieter hint of where things were headed; it was the sweet contact between lovers who were connecting outside the bedroom, too. Holding hands would be some kind of symbol that acknowledged what was happening between them.

And whatever was happening was bound to become far too treacherous for her heart. She felt healed from the loss of her father; she'd made it through, she'd survived, and she'd learned. She lived on the other side of the pain and the grief. That healed heart—such a precious gift that so many people never reached, or took for granted when they did—needed protection, didn't it? The heart could be a fearless creature, prone to parading around town naked and unafraid. It needed the brain to keep it safe from its own propensity for foolish acts.

Even on a temporary basis. Perhaps especially since she and Becker could only be temporary. She didn't want to head north with an aching in her chest from missing him. Because she *would* miss him.

She kept her hand to herself. She kept her heart shielded safely in its cage where it could behave.

When she reached the parking lot, he eyed her motorcycle. "Dangerous beasts. I've seen far too many accidents on bikes." He opened the door of his truck. "Why don't you let me pick you up tomorrow?"

"You'll be my chauffeur, then?"

"Yes."

She gave him the address, he repeated it once, then tapped the side of his head. "Now it's there. In permanent ink."

"Be careful of permanent ink," she warned, and she had a feeling neither one of them was talking about writing implements. Especially when he moved first, brushing away a strand of hair that had dared to flutter across her cheek. The slightest touch from his fingertips lit up her insides, like a neon sign turned on after dark. Her breathing turned shallow as he tucked that hair behind her ear. Then he lowered his hand.

"Be careful on that beast."

"Don't worry. The speedometer is broken, so that makes me go extra slow."

His eyes nearly popped out of his head. "Extra slow?"

"Just kidding. It's just the oil gauge that's broken. Trav is going to help me fix it," she said with a wink.

He narrowed his eyes. "You had me there for a minute."

"I know. It was cute," she said as she pulled on her helmet and straddled the seat, and she couldn't deny how much she liked that he was looking out for her. That she was part of his natural instinct to save and protect.

Chapter Eleven

Becker didn't like the way Megan rode home on her bike. Fine, there was nothing innately daredevilish in her style—she rode at the speed limit, stopped at lights, and didn't weave into oncoming traffic. But he'd tended to enough accidents and been called to the scene of more than he could ever count. Motorcyclists were always the ones who wound up losing when they tangoed in a crash.

In his early days in Chicago, he was the first responder to a motorcycle crash that hadn't even been anyone's fault. As the eyewitnesses told it, the biker had been waiting to make a left turn onto the on-ramp. The light changed, and the biker clipped the curve too wide, bouncing hard, once, twice, three times, on the road. The guy wound up in a back brace for months.

Even as he pulled into his driveway, cut the engine, and headed inside for a quick shower, he couldn't shake the images. Couldn't stop picturing the same thing happening to

Megan. He could even imagine in stark detail being called to the scene—down to the crackle of the scanner and the smell of the gasoline. Then her face, bruised and bloody. He shuddered. He had to halt that image.

He turned the water to scalding, and as it pelted his back, he tried to remind himself that there was no logical reason that he should be so transfixed now on all that could go wrong, with her or with anyone. He'd saved more people along the way than not, and had managed it without feeling like his head was in a vise, forcing him to witness an endless reel of memories. But sometimes, all it took was the flicker of worry, the possibility of someone else he cared for being hurt, or worse, and he was thrust back to the past. Helpless to his wandering mind that returned to the same point in time, hearing the roar of the flames, smelling the burning building, then witnessing the moment the wall killed his friends.

Maybe he could have grabbed them harder. Held on longer.

Fuck if he knew anymore.

All he knew was he hadn't been able to save them. That knowledge was always pounding on his skull, an endless loop that never let up. But then it started to loosen its hold as he returned to her, remembering their morning. When he was with Megan, he didn't feel so caged in. It wasn't that he forgot the past with her; it was that he didn't feel imprisoned by it. For a moment there by the river, with her hand spread out across his chest, fingers stretching over the thin fabric of his T-shirt as if she owned him, he'd felt something like release, like a ghost being exorcised, then quietly slipping away, never to come around again.

Then it was gone.

He scrubbed shampoo in his hair, then rinsed it out, turned the faucet off, and stepped out of the shower. He wrapped a towel around his waist and went hunting through his drawers for clothes. He pulled on boxers, jeans, and a T-shirt. Today, he had to review the books at the Panting Dog, and he hoped the numbers and the rhythm of the balance sheet would soothe his mind.

Until tomorrow. Until he saw her again.

• • •

Megan Photoshopped an ostrich head onto her brother's body. She studied the shot, then added other random animal features — massive black wings to his arms and a pair of webbed feet. Perfect. She emailed it to him, and moments later as her cell phone rang, she prepared herself for some mud-slinging.

But it was her mother calling from the cruise.

"Are you tanned, rested, and ready to come home?" Megan asked when she answered.

"Heck no. Robert and I never want to come back. We're docked somewhere in the Caribbean now, and I'm dining on tilapia and sipping a tropical fruit drink on the deck of a restaurant that looks out over the ocean waves. Have I mentioned it's eighty-two degrees and balmy?"

"It'd better be. It's a cruise in the tropics." She pushed away from her laptop at the kitchen table where she'd been working on the photos.

"How is it being back in town, sweetie?"

"Oh, you know. Same old, same old."

"Could you try being more evasive?" her mom teased,

and Megan liked how playful she seemed. Two weeks at sea under the sun could do that to you. But then, her mom always enjoyed herself when she was with Robert. She had met him when he landed in town and opened a bookstore several years ago, after running a successful one under the same name in New York City. Her mom attended the first reading at the bookstore and a whirlwind courtship followed.

Robert was good to her, treated her like a queen, and was home for dinner every night. Megan figured that's what her mom had wanted most of all. Dependability. In the last year, they'd both scaled back on work, and had a talented manager who ran the shop so they could take vacations like this now and then. It was almost as if her mom was making up for lost time, and cramming all the good things in life into her schedule now, since she'd missed the chance to do so during those dark years.

"It's actually not so bad being back," Megan conceded. "The calendar is keeping me busy. Plus, I've been hanging out with Jamie and Travis. He's still a pain in the ass. That hasn't changed."

"Well, there's not much about your brother we can change, now is there?"

"Truer words were never spoken."

"In any case, I was hoping you could help us out with a little something at the bookstore."

"Sure. What is it?"

"My manager, Craig, needs a day or two off," her mother said. "Could you fill in for him?"

Immediately, Megan cycled back to Jamie's comments the other night about Craig's near-death accident on the slopes. If he needed time off, it probably had to be related to the accident. Besides, Megan's instincts were to help her mom. "Of course. Anything I can do."

"It won't interfere with the photo shoot?"

"Not at all. There's a lot of flexibility with when I can shoot, and I already have a few great shots of the guys, so it's shaping up nicely. Besides, I want to help," Megan said as she headed into the kitchen to root around for something to eat.

Her mother sighed gratefully. "Oh, thank God. Maybe you can stop by the store later this week just to go over everything with Craig? Get up to speed, you know."

"Consider it done."

"He's a sweet guy, too, Megan," her mom said. "You'd like him."

"Are you trying to set me up?"

"He's nice," her mom said, letting her voice trail off suggestively.

Megan rolled her eyes. "Get back to working on your tan."

She didn't need another guy. She needed to figure out what the hell she was doing with *one* guy. The guy she was seeing tomorrow morning.

• • •

The National's latest album played on the sound system as Becker delivered the bar tab to Cara, a well-known dog trainer in town who'd been working with Jamie's new puppy.

"I hear Chance is a perfect pooch," he said as Cara reached into her purse and fished out a few bills for her beer, handing them to Becker.

"He's doing great. Such a fast learner," she said with a

bright smile as Jamie returned from the tables and joined them behind the bar.

"He's the best pup in the universe." Jamie beamed. "And Cara is one disciplined lady. She doesn't let that boy get away with anything."

Cara blushed and ran a hand through her blond hair.

"Don't be shy. You're the best," Jamie said to Cara, wiping her hands on a towel, then scurrying around to wait on another table.

Cara said good-bye, and as she walked out the door, Travis and Smith strolled in. Travis's eyes wandered to Cara, checking her out on his way in, then he snapped his eyes up once she was gone. Becker was tempted to bust him, but decided to keep that bit of intel to himself.

Both men were wearing their blue T-shirts and pants. They were on duty, and were likely here for dinner, which would be on the house as always. They grabbed some empty seats at the bar, and Becker shook hands with each of his men.

"You freeloaders looking for some grub?"

Smith nodded, and Travis flashed a grin. "Oh, please, sir. Can you serve us your best burgers?" Travis asked in a faux-pleading tone.

"Coming right up," he said, and handed the order to Jamie to take to the small kitchen.

"I'll join you," Smith said, pointing his finger to the back of the bar. "Just need to make sure you can find your way back there," he added with a wink.

"Yeah, it's a pretty complicated route," Jamie tossed back, as Smith followed her, leaving Travis alone at the bar, along with a few others.

"How are things on shift today?" Becker poured Travis a Diet Coke and slid it across the counter.

"Bitch of a car accident over on the highway earlier," he answered, shaking his head and blowing out a long stream of air.

Becker's shoulders tightened with worry. "Yeah?"

"Everyone will be fine, but the medics took them to the ER. A few minor broken bones here and there, but the cars took the worst of it."

"The way it should be."

"Absolutely," Travis said, raising his soda in an imaginary toast. "We were there within two minutes. The driver was pretty shaken up but seemed to do better when we arrived."

"Glad to hear," Becker said, feeling a quick rush of warmth over the news that all would be well. That's why they did what they did. To help.

"Hey! Check this out," Travis said, grabbing his phone from his back pocket and sliding his finger across the screen. He scrolled quickly, then called up a picture. "Here's my shot for the calendar."

He took the phone and cracked the hell up. "Man, this is the best picture of you ever taken," he said, admiring the ostrich head on Travis's body.

His friend laughed. "My sister did it."

Becker tensed immediately at the mention of Megan. Travis's sister, his absolutely delicious, adorable, sexy, sweet, kind, and completely forbidden sister. Whom he'd kissed like his life depended on it this morning. And it had. He'd been sure of that at the time.

"You always said she was a hell of a photographer," Becker said quickly, eager to act like all was cool with the situation and he wasn't lusting like a fool over Megan. Besides, he needed to stop. His friendship with Travis meant too much to him, and if anything more happened with Megan, his buddy was not going to be happy. "Looks like she got your best side."

"That she did, bro. That she did," he said, and tucked the phone away. "You're next, right?"

Becker nodded. "Yup. Tomorrow."

"Maybe she'll put a hyena head on you. You'd look mighty fine like that."

"Or an anteater," he offered, glad to keep the conversation light when it came to the woman he couldn't stop thinking about. The woman who calmed his mind and eased the aching in his chest.

They kept up the friendly barbs for another few minutes. Becker should have felt better, because clearly Travis trusted him. But Becker wasn't sure if he trusted himself.

Chapter Twelve

He studied the drawing on the mailbox the next morning. A penguin wearing an orange bow tie clicked his heels, like an old-fashioned movie star singing in the rain. His lips quirked up in curiosity as he leaned in closer for a better look. The penguin was comically drawn, but also precise. There was an expert quality to it, even though the creature wasn't supposed to be the least bit realistic.

Megan's mark on the world.

He was a few minutes early, an old habit that wouldn't die. Being in his line of work entailed so much rushing and quick responding that he'd grown accustomed to getting ready faster than the average man.

"My mom has a thing for penguins."

Becker looked up from Megan's handiwork and tapped the shiny steel box admiringly. "Evidently."

"I drew it for her a few years ago. Well, I sketched it, then painted it." Megan stood on the front porch of a small but well-kept house. The door was painted bright red, and the windows were decorated with planter boxes that were in full bloom with spring flowers in bright yellows and blazing oranges. The two-story house was picturesque, an emerald-green lawn sloping up to meet a brick porch, but the best part was Megan, leaning against the doorjamb, all casual and crazy sexy in a faded denim skirt.

Becker's eyes were drawn to the way the skirt showed off her strong thighs, and then her sculpted calves. Her feet were bare, and as he strolled down the stone path to meet her on the porch, he noticed she had a slender silver ring on her second toe. Becker wasn't a foot man, but for some reason he found the ring inexplicably hot.

Then he met her gaze, and she was smiling, a sweet, almost innocent expression across her beautiful face. When she looked at him like that, he felt a press of nerves inside his chest. It was a strange feeling, and reminded him of picking up a woman for a date for the first time. He hadn't felt this way in ages. He certainly hadn't been celibate in Chicago, by no stretch of the imagination. He'd had lovers and girlfriends, one or two serious, including the one who'd been far more interested in his line of work than an actual relationship, but it had been a while since he'd felt as if he were waiting for a date.

Which was a stupid thought and a dumb feeling, so he locked up both the thought and the feeling in the trunk of things he didn't want to deal with, then threw away the key. He couldn't let himself go there with her or think of her that way. Even after that kiss yesterday. *Especially* after that kiss yesterday.

"I'm no expert on penguin art, but I like your style. It's playful," he said, gesturing to the mailbox.

"Thank you."

"Reminds me of something my brother sent me a few weeks ago from one of the movies he's working on."

"He's working on a penguin movie?" she teased.

He shook his head. "No. An outer space thing. But it's got a comical flair like yours. And I told him as well how much I like it."

"Then that makes me happy," she said and pointed to the open door. "I'm just finishing up breakfast. Want to come in for a second?"

"Sure," he said, glad that he'd battened down the mental hatches before walking into her house. Fine, it wasn't even her home, and it wasn't as if her mom's surroundings would give away much about Megan and who she was beyond the little flashes she'd let him see. But then as she led him into the kitchen, he stopped short when he spotted a framed photo on the wall.

Taken years ago and faded to a sepia shade, the picture was still recognizable. A young Megan and Travis were jumping into a pool with their father. In another shot, they were roasting marshmallows at a campfire. Next, their father was pushing his kids on a swing set. Becker scanned the wall of family photos. The odd thing was all the pictures were of a young Megan and Travis. Then, there was a handful of them older, in their early teens. It was as if years went missing in the family. Becker knew Megan's dad had died when she was young; he and Travis had talked about it. Still, it was sad to see a sort of black hole in the photographic history of the Jansen family.

He left the photos behind and followed Megan into the kitchen, the first rays of morning starting to peek through the windows. She picked up a box of Cinnamon Life cereal and waggled it at him. "Can I interest you in some cereal? I know, I know. Try to contain your enthusiasm at how awesome a cook I am."

His lips quirked into a smile. "You can always interest me in cereal. That's my favorite kind."

"I know," she said, and turned to the cabinet to reach for another bowl.

As he watched her reach into the cupboard, her shirt riding up and showing a sliver of her sexy waist, he latched onto what she'd just said. "How did you know?"

She swiveled back with a maroon ceramic bowl in hand. "Um," she said, and looked down as if she'd been caught red-handed. "I noticed it at your house."

For some reason, this made him smile. It wasn't even so much that she'd noticed, but that she'd remembered.

She poured him a bowl and clinked her spoon to his. "A toast to the best kind of cereal."

"What else did you notice at my house?" he asked as he took a spoonful.

She rolled her eyes. "Nothing," she said, but the red that flooded her cheeks gave her away.

"Go through my sock drawers, too, maybe?"

"No."

"Tupperware?"

"Fine. If you must know, I perused the utensils."

He raised an eyebrow as he took another bite. "Interesting," he said in between crunches. "What did you learn?"

"That you don't have enough teaspoons," she said with a very straight face that made Becker nearly spit out his cereal with laughter.

"But what about butter knives?"

"You have plenty of those."

"How about soup spoons?"

"I better check again. I didn't take a proper inventory of soup spoons."

"Falling down on the job," he teased.

Soon, she finished her cereal, rinsed out the bowl, and left it in the sink. She started putting dishes away in the cupboards as he worked through his cereal. He watched her whip through the dishes like a champion, shelving the plates, then the glasses, then the bowls. She reached for a tall vase next, quickly hoisting herself up onto the counter like an agile creature so she could align the vase on the top of the cupboards. "The cupboards are all full and this is the only place these tall vases fit," she explained as she swiveled around.

She crouched down to hop off the counter, and he immediately pictured her toppling off in a topsy-turvy mess, whacking her head on the dishwasher handle and falling smack on her butt on the floor. Instantly, he thrust his bowl onto the counter, ready to catch. Instead, she moved like a cat, landing softly on her feet.

"I thought you were going to fall. Since you admitted you were a klutz," he said.

She winked. "I just said that to pick you up."

He laughed. "Well, it worked, didn't it?"

"Like a charm. I made you think I was the typical klutzy heroine."

"When in fact, there is nothing typical about you. Did you say anything else to pick me up?"

"I think it was all the things I didn't say that you liked so much," she said, lowering her voice and looking straight at him as he dried off his hands on a towel.

"What do you mean?"

He watched her swallow, as if she were considering what to say. "I think you liked the fact that I didn't tell you chapter, line, and verse. I think you prefer not knowing the details," she said, and her voice sounded thin and nervous. "You liked it better when I wasn't totally myself."

Instinctively, he took a step toward her, running his hand along her arm. He shouldn't be touching her. He shouldn't be speaking so plainly to her about how he felt. But he was having the hardest time acting as if there was nothing between them. They weren't friends, they weren't photographer and subject. They were onetime lovers who wanted to be more, who were trying to hold back. Or maybe trying not to. "That's not true. I like when you share things with me."

"Isn't it, though? You said it was easier when we hardly knew each other," she said, repeating their words from the coffee shop.

Maybe not holding back would yield a greater reward. Because he liked this far too much. Enjoyed it. Craved it. Needed it.

"Yes. I did. And so did you. And it *was* easier," he said, his heart beating faster as he practiced brutal honesty with her. No walls. No secrets. No pretending. "And now it's harder for a million reasons. But I also like knowing who you are. More than I should. Much more than I should," he said, letting his voice trail off as he ran a finger down the bare skin of her arm. They were both watching as she reached for his hand, briefly lacing her fingers through his. That simple touch sent a flurry of shivers down his spine. "I like knowing about your owl. And your tattoo dreams. And I like knowing about the river and what it means to you. And I like knowing you're not really a klutz."

"But what if I were?" she said with a twinkle in her eyes. "What if I had fallen off the counter and hit my head on the cupboard door?"

"Then I'd have caught you in seconds," he said, letting go of her hand. "And wrapped an arm around your shoulder," he added, demonstrating. "Then this." He scooped her up in his arms, carrying her as he walked across the kitchen.

"Show-off!" she said, and pounded her fists playfully against his chest.

"What? You thought I couldn't lift you?"

"I knew you could. I just didn't expect you to."

"Ah, so I surprised you."

"Yes. You did."

"Good. Because I suspect that's not easy to do," he said as he set her down in the living room.

"You're strong," she said.

"I'm supposed to be. Comes with the job."

"I know. I'm just not used to being carried. Travis was always trying to toss me on his shoulder and carry me just because he could, but I didn't let him."

"But you let me."

"You're more fun to be carried by," she said, her brown eyes sparkling. *Fun.* He didn't think anyone had called him fun in a long, long time. Hearing it from Megan tugged at his heart. "Besides, when he tried to carry me I just ran away from him," she said softly. The implication was thick in the air that she hadn't run from him.

"Because you're Miss Independent."

"Am I?" she asked, arching an eyebrow.

"As far as I can tell."

"Does that make you crazy?"

"Nearly everything about you does," he said, his lips quirking up. "Now, you want to get some shoes on and I'll clean the kitchen for you?"

Her eyes lit up as if he'd won a teddy bear for her at the fair. But maybe cleaning up the kitchen was her version of a teddy bear.

"Thank you. I'll be right back."

He returned to the kitchen, washed the breakfast dishes, tucked the cereal box onto its shelf, then met Megan at the door. She wore black combat boots with her short skirt, and even though he found himself missing that toe ring, she was even hotter with bare legs and badass boots.

"You have everything? Bunker pants, suspenders, boots, helmet?" she asked.

"Back of the truck. Like you asked. And you? What's in that tackle box?" Becker said, tipping his forehead to the black metal container she carried that looked suspiciously as if it might be home to fishing lures. "Don't get me all excited and tell me we're really going fishing."

When they reached his truck and he opened the passenger door to let her in, she flashed him a devious grin, then said, "Makeup. Makeup and body paint."

That was all he could think about on the drive to the river.

Body paint, and all its possible meanings.

He wanted to paint her body red. Paint it black. Paint it with his hands. Paint it with his tongue. He gripped the wheel hard, forcing himself to focus on the road as he drove.

But once they reached their destination, he had to admit he was damn curious what she intended to do to *him* with the body paint.

Chapter Thirteen

"I thought you were going for a more natural look and feel to the calendar. Now what? Are you going to paint a fire on my chest?" Becker asked after they reached the bend in the river that Megan had declared the perfect photographic backdrop. The spot was secluded, hugged by overhanging willow branches that formed a canopy over the water. They were in a narrow valley, surrounded only by the gurgling river, the chirping of birds, and the misty fog that rolled through on its way out as the sun rose overhead.

"It won't be tacky, I promise," she said. "Now sit."

She pointed to a large rock near the river, close to the one they'd perched on yesterday. Becker followed her orders. She opened the black metal box, pursed her lips, and scanned the jars of makeup and tubes of body paint.

Becker tapped his cheek. "How about a tiger? You know, like you're face-painting at a fair."

She grabbed a brush and brandished it like a weapon,

wagging it at him. "You better watch it, or I'll give you a but-terfly or a ladybug," she said with narrowed eyes.

He held up his hands in surrender. "I'll keep my mouth shut."

"You do that."

She selected a tube of charcoal gray paint, a slate-colored one, then midnight black. "Besides, this'll be easy. I once did a shoot in L.A. for this antifur ad campaign. I worked with another artist to paint the models to look like animals. Took a few hours. This will only be a few minutes."

"I trust this washes off easily?"

She rolled her eyes. "Of course. And it's nontoxic and all that."

She opened a jar and dipped a paintbrush into it, swirl-ing the bristles into the charcoal color. "Take your shirt off," she said. He reached over his shoulder and removed the blue shirt easily in one swift move, revealing the broad chest that would now be her canvas.

Her breath fled as she took in the sight of his muscled body. The rippling abs, the carved pecs, and the beautifully broad shoulders. She reminded herself she had a job to do, so she moved closer, considering the best position for paint-ing him. Should she stand between his legs, straddle a thigh, or paint from the side leaning over?

"Um, I kinda think I need to get a little closer."

"Be my guest," he said, and waited for her to make a move.

She opted for straddling him, inching closer so one strong thigh was between her bare legs. He wore the heavy beige turnouts, but even through the thick fabric, she could feel the flexed muscle of his quad between her legs. Why had she thought painting him would be a good idea? Why had she picked this deserted location? Was it subconscious or had she deliberately done this so she'd fall into another moment with him without a soul around to see them?

She hadn't been doing such a good job resisting him these last twenty-four hours. Even when she texted him the other night, she could pretend that interaction was safe, since it consisted only of words. But words started everything. Their whole connection began with a conversation that had unfurled into more. She loved the effect she seemed to have on him, how he seemed freer, happier, less tightly wound with her. She'd never been able to do a thing for Jason. But in a mere week in town, she'd already felt like she mattered. She wanted that—she craved that.

Even so, more contact would be dangerous. It would be stoking the fire that was all too ready to roar. She could already see herself with him in so many ways, but being with a man like him would only ever amount to getting hurt.

Right?

Or maybe it wouldn't, a tiny little voice suggested.

She shushed that voice as the hem of her short skirt inched up farther. *Focus*, she told herself.

Starting at his belly button, she painted a faint line of gray up and over the hard ladder of his stomach, the brush moving and bending with the planes of his body. She dipped the brush into another jar and edged the color with a darker hue. He pressed his hands against the rock, gripping it as she painted more color over his muscles. This time, she started at his pecs, swirling the slate gray downward, farther, until she stopped at the waistband of his pants. He inhaled sharply and dug his hands into the rock as if he could rip off pieces of it.

She leaned back to consider her work, then sighed

heavily. It was all wrong. It looked affected, like stylized plumes of smoke. She'd envisioned a realistic look, as if he'd truly just emerged from battling a smoky forest fire.

"I need to mix it in better. I need to use my hands."

He didn't reply. He only nodded as she laid the brush on the rock. This time she settled over both his legs, sitting across them, his firm thighs holding her. He bit out a curse when she placed her hands on his chest.

"I just want it to look right," she said breathily.

"Yeah," he said, staying still. He was a wall, immovable. He was the embodiment of rigid resistance as she feathered a hand over his chest. But two things gave him away. His breathing that grew louder, more intense. And the huge bulge in his pants that pressed against her inner thigh.

The feel of his hard-on was almost enough to cloud her brain and make her toss her paints and makeup and camera somewhere behind her, letting them fall amid the crisp leaves and fallen twigs. To say: *fuck me now, please. Fuck me now and put us both out of our misery. Bring us both to the edge, and then shove me over the cliff into ecstasy.*

Just the thought of what his hard length could do to her threatened to annihilate all her self-control. Because whatever she had left was draining away as the throbbing between her legs increased. She was so close she could rub against him. She could press the damp triangle of her white thong underwear against his pants and probably get herself off just from the friction.

But she had a job to do, and she needed to do it well, so she could move on to Portland and begin her dream job. She rubbed her hands across his steely frame, smudging the body paint until it at last looked a bit like the remnants of smoke, like a brave man had beaten back raging flames. Protected the forest, protected the people, protected the whole damn town and emerged unscathed, with just the dust and dirt sticking to his sweaty, hot chest.

Tension roiled between them like an electrical wire as she worked. The tightness in his body was a magnet. She breathed deeply, holding in all her desires, all her instincts to press her body against his. When she finished, she scooted back, held up her charcoal-smudged hands, and pronounced, "Done."

"Your hands are dirty," he said in a hoarse voice.

"Very dirty," she murmured, and she wasn't talking about her hands anymore.

His eyes strayed to the T-shirt he'd tossed to the ground. "Can you grab my shirt?"

"Yes," she said and twisted down to reach for his T-shirt. She handed it to him.

He took the fabric and used it as a cloth to wipe the paint off her hands. "Now, I'm going to need you to remember this position. Can you do that for me?" he asked in a commanding tone that thrummed through her body.

"Yes."

He tipped his forehead to the water.

"This is the real money shot now. Because when you take a picture of me, I am going to have so much fucking lust in my eyes from how much I want you right now."

Hot desire pulsed through her blood from his words. She wanted him, too. Desperately. Her body was molten, her skin sizzling from head to toe. She shifted off of him, readjusting her skirt. He rose and walked to the water, lapping the rocks on the bank of the riverbed. She reached into her camera bag, slung her Nikon over her neck, and headed for the water.

She brought the viewfinder to her eye and felt a bit like a proud film director. The shot was perfect. The setting, the wooded trees, the morning light. But most of all—him. The desire in his eyes was tangible. Even in the bulky, heavy turnouts, she could make out the shape of his hard length. The pants were thick enough that the shot wasn't too dirty, but he was still visible enough that he was perfect fodder— he was the firefighter every woman fantasized about.

That was the trouble. He made her feel too good, and it wasn't a fantasy; it was all too real. More real than she ever expected. She should draw some lines in the sand with him and make a strong pact to behave. But she didn't want him to keep his hands off her. She wanted his hands, his head, his heart.

After she finished shooting, she peered through the LCD screen to confirm she had enough shots. Then she heard him walking to her, and his nearness stirred her blood.

"Put the camera down, Megan," he said.

Surprised by his command, she glanced up, the camera still in her grip. His eyes were full of dark craving, rimmed with black around the pupils. He didn't stop looking at her, nor did he break the hold he had on her as he spoke again in a low and husky voice.

"You have ten seconds to put down the camera and get back into the same position I asked you to remember."

All the air whooshed out of her lungs from the dominating way he talked to her, leaving her no choice but to return to the rock. He sat down and pulled her onto him. She swallowed, her throat dry as he stared at her as if he wanted to consume her.

"Now touch yourself."

She exhaled hotly, overcome with desire. Her entire being had been reduced to the aching between her legs. Even so, she managed a weak protest. "I thought we agreed…"

"I don't care what we agreed to. I can't fight this anymore, and I can't pretend I don't want you in every way. You are under my skin, and in my head, and even if there are one million reasons or just one reason not to touch you, I can't find it in me right now to resist."

"I can't either," she said, and the admission was a huge relief. The tension was too much to bear. She was a cog wound too tight in danger of snapping. She'd rather bend. *With him.*

"Torture me, Megan, with your sexy sounds," he growled. "I want to watch you and see the look on your face when you're close to breaking. I want to hear those sounds you make when you're losing control," he said, and she trembled from his words. "Do you want to come right now as much as I want to watch you?"

"More than anything."

Dipping his hands under her skirt, he hiked it up to her waist, exposing her to him with only the thin triangle between her legs covering her. His fingers slid inside her panties, and she moaned so loudly she was sure the birds would start talking back to her, joining her in a chorus of cries. He pushed the fabric to the side. Then he held on to her hips, leaving the work up to Megan.

"Now, it's your turn."

She brought her fingers between her legs. She traced her own wetness, rubbing the slickness across her core, his eyes growing hungrier as he watched her. Her fingers stroked up and down, slowly at first, but then she started to quicken her pace. She arched her back, and at the same time, he used one hand to push up her shirt above her breasts. He unhooked her bra in seconds, and one big hand cupped a breast, kneading and massaging as she rubbed.

"Now bring some right here," he instructed, squeezing the tight peak of her nipple. She gave him a strange look. "You painted me. Now paint yourself and let me taste it."

A shock wave of pleasure rocked her at the request. Her face grew hotter, her need for him more intense. She dipped her index finger between her legs and then circled it around one breast.

He growled as he leaned into her, sucking her own juices from her hard nipple. She cried out at the sensation, then he pulled back just as quickly, trailing a strong, calloused finger from her sternum to her belly. "Now here. Paint yourself here."

She nodded quickly, wanting to keep touching herself, to rub faster and harder, to spread her legs and cry out. But she resisted, instead following his artistic direction to spread the evidence of her desire in a line from her belly to her breasts. Then he dived in for another long, lingering slide of his tongue across her skin.

"You're killing me."

He tucked his face in the crook of her neck, rubbing his jaw against her shoulder and finding her ear so he could whisper, "Paint yourself. One more time. For me."

"Where?" she said in a ragged breath, unsure where her voice was even coming from anymore. How she was forming words. Maybe she was powered solely by want.

"Here." He drew a line from her neck to the hollow of her throat.

She slid her fingers back between her legs where she was so wet now she could probably have painted her entire body for him. She did as asked, and then shuddered at the feel of his tongue retracing the same path. He moaned deeply as he tasted her, murmuring, "So good. So fucking good." Then his lips brushed the hollow of her throat, a soft kiss, but full of heat as he sucked the last remaining traces.

"Now show me how you fuck yourself."

Tension swelled inside her. Her hand returned to between her legs, and she expertly moved her fingers as he held on to her hips, letting her lean back and let go.

"Come for me, Megan. Let me watch you get off."

His words drove her on, and soon she felt her belly tighten, once, twice, three times, and her legs were shaking, and a massive wave slammed into her as he pushed her long hair away from her face and breathed into her neck. "Come for me on your hand."

That did it. She shattered, blinding waves of pleasure flooding her body, her bones, and her skin. Every part of her was alive and pulsing, from a runaway orgasm that didn't stop. It sped through, spilling into every corner of her body, until finally she could open her eyes and look at Becker. His lips were parted and he grasped her wrist, bringing her fingers to his mouth, sucking off the taste of her until he'd licked every last drop. His dark eyes were heated, and hungry, as if he'd never consumed anything he wanted this much before.

When she finally started to come down from the high, she didn't know what to say, how to act. But he did.

"We need to go. If we stay here any longer, I will tear your clothes off, and the last thing I want is for you to return home naked."

Chapter Fourteen

The house wasn't far from the river. They were both quiet as they slid into his truck, shut the doors, and cruised away from the hiking trails, heading onto the curvy road that led back into Hidden Oaks. The silence was thick, clinging to them like a fine film of dust. They both knew it was time to talk. It was a moment for manning up. A heady kiss in the woods after one night together could be written off as a onetime relapse. Even a few naughty texts were nothing to get all riled up about.

However, what happened today had to be addressed. He'd let it go too far. He'd been driven solely by his desire for her, abandoning all sense of right and wrong. And in so doing, they'd reached a crossroads. He didn't know where they were going or where he wanted to go. But he knew this—neither one of them seemed to have a wink of interest in stopping.

He was about to speak when she went first.

"I'd like to say that we can't keep doing this, but I think we've established we *are* doing this," she offered, and her tone was both serious and wry. A clear-cut acknowledgment of what was transpiring between them.

Becker kept his eyes on the road. He wished they weren't in agreement. He wished they weren't so in sync. He wished he could give her everything she deserved. He wished he'd never met her. Except, he didn't wish that at all. "Saying we should stop is pointless, since we won't? Or we can't?"

"Both. It seems we're still on plan A. We're doing what we planned to do after we first slept together."

"And then what we said we weren't going to do," he added. "Plan B."

"Exactly. But we're not following the new plan."

"Which means all we're doing is skirting the line. Saying we're not getting involved, then doing it anyway."

"Right," she said, raising her voice in emphasis. "We agreed not to do anything else. That it was a onetime thing. And we just can't keep—" She stopped to shake her head in amusement. "Jesus. Look at us. A grown man and woman and we're running off to the goddamn woods to make out."

He chuckled at the way she'd put it. Perfectly. "And then you can't keep your hands off me in the woods. Even though you left me blue-balled," he added, and she laughed deeply at his take on events, since he'd chosen to walk away before it went further. "But I don't care because I like knowing you enjoyed yourself," he said, placing one hand on her bare thigh and running his rough fingers across her smooth skin. She shivered lightly from his touch.

Sure, he was left hanging sexually, but it didn't matter. Being with her soothed him. Her laughter, her forthright nature, her stories from the mud pies to the owl that watched over her, banished the constant rattle and hum in his head. They were gone in the way she knew his favorite cereal, they were gone in the way she asked him why he became a fire-fighter, and they were gone in the way she couldn't mask herself with him. She'd tried that first night, tried so damn hard to only reveal so much. But the more time he spent with her, the more she shared. And today, it had simply been how much she wanted him.

As much as he wanted her.

She turned to him with narrowed eyes that hinted of laughter. Then seriousness. "No, Becker. I can't keep my hands off you. And that's the problem. Let's be grown-ups and figure out what we're doing, even if I'm only here for another week."

The thought flashed by—what if they went back to plan A? Made a go of things for the week or so while she was here? Would that *really* hurt his friendship with Travis? Their relationship had an expiration date, so how could they hurt each other? He could surely convince Travis that a few days was nothing to worry about. Right? While he could sneak around with Megan for the rest of her brief stay, Travis none the wiser, Becker wasn't that kind of guy. He wasn't going to pursue even a casual fling without being on the up-and-up with his buddy. To do anything less would be wrong.

"I agree. So why don't I talk to Travis—"

But the rest of the words were cut off when they turned the corner and spotted Travis in the driveway of their mom's house. Becker's chest constricted at the sight of his friend leaning against the hood of his Jeep. He had to strip himself of all emotions, all feelings, anything that would reveal what he'd done or how he felt about his buddy's little sister.

Megan shot him a quick, nervous look.

"Let's pick this up later and figure things out, okay?" he said, and she nodded as they pulled into the driveway. "I'll call you tonight."

Right now it was time to shut the hell up, and the fact that he was lying to his buddy was like swallowing a stone, and about as uncomfortable. He hoped to hell his feelings weren't written on his face, but he was practiced in stoicism. Was Megan a good actor too, though? Another wave of self-loathing rolled through him for even wishing she could pull off a poker face. He cut the engine, and they hopped out of his truck. Music played from the Jeep's radio. Travis was singing along, tapping out the rhythm with his hands on the hood of the car.

"Where were you guys? Hard at work shooting the calendar?" he asked, and the tension flared again inside Becker. The question was a slingshot back to reality. This was his job—to look out for his guys. To take care of his men. To set a fucking example. Not to sneak around with his friend's sister. Didn't matter if this was temporary with Megan.

Travis was like a brother to him. He was his family, in a way, here in Hidden Oaks, and a damn important part of why this town had started to feel like a new home to him. Because of people like Travis and all the guys he worked with. He'd toyed with giving up the work after the fire in Chicago, but he hadn't been able to walk away from the firehouse. His future was set in stone from the moment his brother broke his arm when they were kids. He was a fireman and that wasn't changing. That meant he could never give Megan what she deserved. The promise of coming home.

But they could have this much—the rest of her time here. They both wanted more; they should make the most of the short time, like a vacation on a beautiful island, where you soak up the sun every second of the day. He had to do this right and man up. Come clean with Travis. But before he did that, he needed to finish his conversation with Megan and now was clearly not the time.

"Just shooting my close-up. It's better than yours," Becker said, segueing into their familiar ribbing. Anything to cover up the way he was feeling about Travis's sister. Becker sneaked a glance at Megan, and her features were tight, her jaw set.

"What are you doing here?" she asked.

"I'm going down to Monterey later for an executive game. I came over to fix the oil gauge on your bike. Told you I would. You already forgot?"

"Oh, right. Thank you," she said to her brother with relief in her voice. "I definitely need you to fix that. And then I have to go help at the bookstore later today."

"Let's get cracking, then," Travis said, patting the seat of her motorcycle.

That heavy knot loosened as he watched them. Megan could take care of herself. She was strong and independent, and had a family who loved her and looked out for her. She didn't need him to be anything more than the here and now, and that was fine by him. For now, he could lose himself in the work tonight at the bar, and let the Panting Dog do its job occupying front and center in his brain. Then he'd talk to Travis and show him his cards.

Chapter Fifteen

Megan tossed a tennis ball across the small backyard and the puppy scampered across the grass in hot pursuit. Megan had stopped by Jamie's on the way to the bookstore. She had contemplated telling her all about Becker the morning after their first night, but once Megan knew who he was, there was no need.

Now there was a definite need, a huge, gaping need, so she'd come over and confessed everything, from the first night they spent together, to Travis's concerns, to the river.

"Good boy!" Jamie shouted, cheering the pup. "Bring it back."

Chance tore across the lawn, arriving in front of Jamie. "Now drop," she told him and he obeyed, depositing the ball at his mistress's feet.

"He's a quick learner," Megan observed, as Jamie tossed another ball.

Jamie winked and snapped her fingers. "I like to keep

my men in line."

"Ha. No problem on that with Smith. He's crazy about you."

"The feeling is one hundred percent mutual," Jamie said and smiled so wide that Megan figured a family of four could drift out to sea on that smile. Jamie and Smith were so ridiculously in love that Megan could hardly believe there was ever a time when they were unsure about each other. "But enough about me. What are we going to do about you and my boss? And can I just say I still can't believe you hooked up with him! With my *boss.*"

She shot Jamie a narrow look. "I hardly think him being your boss is the issue here. It's sort of the other thing he is."

Jamie shrugged wistfully, then lobbed another tennis ball across the yard. "I know. Your brother's friend, not to mention a firefighter."

She held her hands out wide. "I know. That's sort of the problem."

Jamie wagged a finger and adopted a serious tone. "*No men who face mortal danger on a daily basis.*"

"Well, it's kind of understandable, don't you think?"

"Sure. But hell, it's Hidden Oaks. There aren't that many fires here. I guess that's why I don't worry too much about Smith."

But Megan knew better. The reason Jamie wasn't plagued with the same fears was how she was raised. Jamie grew up with a mom and a dad who were madly in love and still were to this day. Her parents ran a local vineyard together. She saw them regularly, had dinner with the pair of them. Megan didn't expect her to understand why she feared traveling the romance route with a firefighter because Jamie hadn't grown up seeing what that life might lead to. All that sadness. All those broken nights, punctuated by tears and heavy sighs. A canyon's worth of missing someone who would never come back.

"You honestly never worry about something happening to Smith?" she asked, pressing the issue as she took her turn scooping up the ball for the dog, then tossing it for him. He was a puppy; his energy was boundless.

"Sure. I didn't mean to make light of it. Of course, anything can happen at any time. But that's true for anyone. No one is immune to the possibility of loss, no matter what the job is. And as for Smith being a firefighter, well, the fact that he does what he does is part of why I love him so much."

Megan let the weight of those words sink in. Even though she worried immensely about her brother, she also admired him deeply. Because he was brave. He didn't just play the hero. He *was* a hero. The same was true of Becker; running into a burning house to save strangers was courageous. There were no ifs, ands, or buts about it. Truth be told, it was part of what she was liking so much about Becker. She hadn't expected to fall for that side of him; she'd thought she could rope it off and keep his job at a distance, but deep down, her heart was melting for all of him.

Damn heart. Damn annoying, frustrating heart. It was supposed to have barriers, to protect her from this kind of feeling. But instead of fighting it off from the outside, she was falling from the inside.

She shooed away those thoughts to focus on Jamie. "I remember that time you called me when you were still unsure of things with Smith. I'm so happy that you guys are together and in love." She wrapped an arm around Jamie and pulled her in for a quick hug.

"Me, too." They pulled apart when Chance nosed Jamie's leg. She stroked his snout and cooed at him, then continued the ball-throwing. "Can I tell you something funny?"

"Sure. I could use a laugh."

"This is going to sound crazy, but I once pictured you with Becker. I had a hunch that you two might be good for each other."

"I remember you telling me he was *super hot*, and you sure as hell weren't lying about that."

"There's more to it, though. One night when I was at the bar, all mixed up about Smith and how I felt about him, I was missing you and wishing I could talk to you, and it hit me. You're so good at that. At just talking to people, and being straightforward and getting to the heart of things. And it made me think you might be good together. I think he's afraid of commitment, too."

"I'm not afraid of commitment. I was with Jason for almost two years. I was so committed I was beyond committed," Megan said defensively.

"That's not what I mean. What I mean is he's lost people too, Megan. He doesn't talk about it, but it's kind of this unspoken thing. He moved here because there was some terrible fire in Chicago where he used to work, and he lost a bunch of his men."

Tears pricked the backs of her eyes. "Oh, no."

Jamie nodded. "I think it's pretty hard for him to even think about being involved with someone for that reason. I mean, it's not like he tells me this. I'm just using my woman's intuition. But he's a loner. He's very focused on his business, and his job, and I've always thought it's because he knows what getting close could lead to."

To loss. To the worst kind of heartbreak you could imagine. "How on earth does that make me perfect for him then?"

"Because," Jamie said, her voice rising in emphasis. "Because you've made it to the other side. He needs someone who can show him that life isn't always painful. That getting close isn't always scary. He's not afraid of commitment because he's a playboy or a jerk. He's afraid because he thinks he's too damaged. Sometimes, a man like that needs a woman like you to show him the other side, because you're tough and strong and a survivor. Because you tell it like it is. You tell yourself you have all these rules and you don't date firemen or men who have dangerous jobs, but you chase your dreams. You went to L.A. for Jason. You're going to Portland to become a tattoo artist. You aren't afraid."

"Okay, so you think I'm perfect for him. But tell me why he's perfect for me then?"

"Because he is incredibly caring, and smart and sensitive. And ultimately, because he is *good*."

"It's that simple?"

"Sometimes it is. Oh, but wait. There's one part I can't answer. How was the — " Jamie asked, then waggled her eyebrows.

She sighed, and butterflies threatened to take her chest hostage from the memories. "It was epic. It was out of this world." Megan's gaze drifted off; her eyes went glassy as she flashed back to their first night. "It was like he knew me. Like he knew my body. It was like he'd been wanting to do things to me for ages and finally had the chance. Which sounds crazy, considering we just met. But that's what it felt like. We had this intense physical connection."

"And now there's an emotional connection. So what are

you going to do about Travis? And what are you going to do about the fact that you're leaving?"

"I'm going to take it one thing at a time. Travis made it pretty damn clear I needed to stay the hell away, and I love him and respect him and want to do right by him."

"But you're not doing right by him by sneaking around. If you're not going to follow his advice, you should at least be honest and let him know that you respect him, but you're choosing your own way."

As she walked to her mom's store, she knew that Jamie was right. Her brother had raised her better than this. If she was going to keep falling into Becker's arms while she was here, she had to tell her brother.

An Open Book had been a part of her life since high school, when her mom met and married Robert. She'd spent many days and evenings here, helping out on weekends, and now and then during college when she came home during breaks. She wasn't a bookish kid growing up, though she did love the escape of a good story, preferably an adventure tale involving spies, high-stakes getaways, and epic kisses in sophisticated foreign cities.

Whenever she was here she spent most of her time in the kids' section, reconnecting with the books that sparked her love of drawing in the first place—the illustrated tales that had hooked her when she was younger.

Megan pulled open the door and headed over to the counter, recognizing Craig immediately from the crutches. He was busy at the register. When he finished with a customer, he turned to her.

"Hey. I'm Megan Jansen," she said, then gave a quick wave, knowing it would be easier for him than having to shake hands.

He flashed a bright smile. He had a certain California charm about him, with tousled blond hair, light blue eyes, and a trim build.

"Good to meet you. Glad you could help out."

"It's my pleasure. I'm ready for my refresher course, and I know you have to leave soon," Megan said, and walked behind the counter, standing next to Craig. He opened a drawer, keeping himself impressively steady with his crutches. "You're a pro at those," she said.

"Ha. Thanks. Was always one of my life's aspirations to master crutches."

"How much longer?"

"I should get rid of the cast this week, actually. That's why I needed you to fill in so I can see the ortho surgeon for a check-in. But I'll have the crutches for another eight weeks. And then probably at least a year of PT."

Her eyes widened. "That is a long time," she said, with sympathy in her voice.

He nodded. "My leg was broken in several places, and this kind of break usually takes more time than usual. It was a hell of a fall, turned out."

"I heard some of the details, but may I ask what happened? Jamie said that you were training for some sort of charity race?"

"Yep. The annual MS fund-raiser. My sister has MS, so I always do the race to raise money for research. On one of my last training races, there was a crazy skier not paying attention and shooting downhill like a bat out of hell. Trouble was, the skier was aiming straight for a young kid on a snowboard. I saw the kid, grabbed the back of his jacket to pull him out of harm's way, then wound up careening down the slope myself."

"Wow," she said, breathing out low and shaking her head.

"Pretty sure I toppled about twenty times."

"I'm so sorry, Craig. That sucks. How's the kid doing?"

Craig smiled brightly, his grin lighting up his whole face. "He's good. Perfect. Not a hair on his head out of place."

"Well, there's that."

"His parents keep sending me gifts every week. It's kind of cute. The kid even wrote me a card."

"What about the guy? The skier?"

Craig shook his head, his shaggy blond hair brushing against his forehead. "Gone. Just kept on skiing. Probably took another run, too."

"Crazy," she said, shaking her head sympathetically. She felt bad for Craig. Just a regular guy trying to help his sister. And it wasn't even his fault, but he was the one who stepped in to save the day in a hit-and-run. Funny how life worked out like that.

"What can you do?" Craig said, but he didn't sound sad. "Things happen and you just gotta deal. Let me show you how to run this bad boy."

He spent the next fifteen minutes reviewing the high-level details for her—ringing up purchases, cash versus credit, and handling gift cards. Megan paid attention, even though the whole time she was thinking of how even a guy who managed a bookshop could get hurt. How there were no guarantees. That life didn't offer you any safety nets.

She worked until closing time, then locked the door and took a deep breath. She checked her phone, hoping for a text from Becker as he'd promised, but there was none. She wasn't going to let that bother her. She had the store to herself for a while and she was going to enjoy her time alone. She wandered through the aisles, past the shelves in thrillers, mysteries, poetry, and nonfiction, too. There were a few empty shelves in one corner of the store near the small coffee bar; her mom had hired Smith to start building out a larger cafe. Megan strolled past it, picturing an expanded array of cookies, cakes, and other goodies. She meandered to her favorite spot—the kids' section, where she ran her hands across several picture books, and after careful consideration, picked one starring a giraffe.

Positioning the book on a thimble-sized chair as if it were an easel, she lay back in one of the multicolored bean bags. She removed her leather bracelets so they wouldn't get in the way, placing them next to her on the soft, form-less chair. She grabbed her sketchbook from her cavernous purse, along with the colored pencils she'd brought along for the occasion, and spent the next few hours drawing varia-tions on this giraffe.

Her favorite was the one where the giraffe wore a red wig.

She hadn't had as much time to draw when she was in Los Angeles. Tending to Jason's problems had taken its toll on her and sapped her of her creativity.

As the clock neared midnight, she packed up, musing to

herself on how nice it was to be free of him—physically *and* mentally. Jason was finally in the past. The strangling year of trying to help him had loosened its hold. How weird that only one month ago, she was in Los Angeles knotted and twisted over him. What to do, how to leave, what to say. Most of all, should she keep trying?

That's why she'd stayed with him so long, despite his addiction. She'd wrestled with her own responsibility to someone like him. Should she abandon him when he needed someone most? Yet Jason had never truly needed her. He needed his drug, and that was the problem. He had never admitted he *had* a problem, and maybe if he had she would have stayed longer or tried harder. As it was, she simply felt free now. Being with him had been a long, slow suffocation. Caring for someone who didn't care one bit about changing was like being frayed thin. He hadn't wanted what she had to give.

She wasn't really sure what it would be like to be with someone who did want what she had to give. But she'd felt a flicker of it with Becker. There was the right kind of give-and-take between them. They seemed to almost fit, as if all her lost and missing parts aligned with him, and vice versa.

She checked her phone once more. Still nothing. That was a bummer. She'd been hoping to hear from him. To reconnect and figure out what the hell they were doing next, even if it was only for a few more days.

She adjusted her skirt, shelved the book, grabbed her bags, put her leather bracelets back on, and left the store, locking up. On the walk to her bike, she noticed most of the lights in the Panting Dog were out except one. She wasn't the type of woman to sit around and wait for a man. Her feet took her straight to the window, where she saw him on the other side, bent over a laptop, pushing a hand through his hair, staring hard at the screen.

She didn't want to ignore her feelings anymore. She wanted to see him. She wanted to know him more. She wanted them to do the right thing. She tapped on the window and was greeted by a look that said he'd been missing her, that he'd been hoping she'd come by.

He rose and walked to the door. His deep brown eyes were dark and intense, and he looked at her as if he wanted to consume her and take care of her at the same time. He was beautiful in his jeans and a button-down shirt that begged to be undone. She'd only seen him in T-shirts and jeans, or T-shirts and running shorts, but here he was in a sort of California business casual, and the clothes fit him so well that it seemed a sin to take them off. But she was willing to commit that sin. Oh yes, she was willing.

"Hi," she said as he held open the door. Her voice didn't sound nervous or small. It sounded certain, like how she felt.

"Hi," he said, and his tone mirrored hers. "Want a beer?"

Another nod.

He closed the door and locked it. She followed him, joining him behind the counter as he wrapped a hand around the tap. She dropped her purse on the bar.

"Good song," she said, as she pointed to the speakers playing Kings of Leon.

"Good album. Can I interest you in a Labrador?"

"Yes."

He poured two glasses, and she took a quick sip of her beer, barely tasting it, because she was elsewhere. She was several minutes ahead, picturing them tangled up in each other, not able to get enough. Life was short. Anything could happen at any time. Sometimes, you had to seize the moment and savor it for as long as it lasted. "You didn't text, so I figured your phone must be broken," she said, her lips curving up in a grin.

"My phone isn't broken," he said, a small smile tugging at the corners of his mouth. "But I'm glad you're here."

"You are?"

He nodded and stepped closer to her. The physical proximity to him was dizzying, but there was more than that between them now. She swore she could see the emotions starting to show themselves, like the shimmer of a mirage visible under the desert sun. "I didn't write to you because I don't know what the fuck to do. You're leaving town soon, and I can't give you what you deserve, and I can't stand the thought of sabotaging my friendship with your brother," he said, and she heard the barrenness in his voice, but the bone-deep fear too. Then his tone shifted and softened as his gaze hooked on hers. "But you're here, and that's all I can seem to think about. Because even when you're not here, you're all I can seem to think about anyway."

"I am?" she asked, and her blood stirred.

"Yes," he said, never breaking her gaze, never looking away. She read his eyes, and she knew he didn't just want her; he needed her. In the barest whisper, he added, "With you, it always seems to be yes."

She licked her lips once, breathed out, put the glass down. She didn't want to resist, so she clasped her hands tightly around his neck, crushing his lips with hers. She took him by surprise, and he didn't seem to mind. She had a crazy feeling that he needed her at times to take control, to force him to let go of all the damn restraint he held on to, that he *needed* someone to blindfold him, tie him up, pin him down, and take him there.

He groaned as she kissed harder, deeper, damn near ready to go for broke.

So she did. She shoved him against the counter, no easy feat considering his size. But she'd caught him off guard, and she liked that. With quick hands, she undid the button on his jeans, then the zipper.

He inhaled sharply as she teased at the waistband of his boxer briefs.

"Let me," she said in a breathy voice.

"You think I was going to stop you?"

"I don't know. Just don't. Don't stop me."

"Don't you get it? I can't stop with you, Megan. I can't."

She reached a hand inside his boxer briefs, thrilling at the feel of him in her hands once more.

Chapter Sixteen

"Fuck," he said in a strangled voice as she stroked him. He'd never been harder; he'd never wanted a woman this badly. As her soft fingers wrapped around him, all his thoughts drained away, all the tension spun out of his body, and this was all there was. He'd pictured this plenty of times and he'd craved it so damn much. Her touch, her hands, her lips. He loved getting her off, but he didn't stand a chance right now of doing anything else but taking what she planned to give.

That was fine by him.

He leaned against the bar, the hard wood digging into his back like it was cutting him, but he didn't fucking care at all, because there was nothing that mattered right now more than Megan, and the way she dropped to her knees, pulled down his briefs, and brought him to her lips.

He was so used to being in control, but he didn't want control right now. He wanted to let go. He never took his eyes off her, watching her gorgeous face and her delicious lips as she teased him at first, trailing her tongue from the head to the base, then back up again.

He groaned and grabbed her hair, twining his fingers through those beautiful brown strands as she dived back in, licking him like he was a piece of candy, and fuck if that wasn't the hottest thing in the whole damn world. She cupped his balls in her palm and teased her tongue along his dick. An incinerating heat ricocheted through his bones, to his blood, into every cell in his body. He wanted to thrust into her mouth. But he let her lead, let her set the pace. Didn't matter. She could have him all the way in, or just blaze those succulent trails with her wicked tongue, and he'd come just the same.

She pulled back, kissing the head, then looked up at him. "You taste good." She sounded as if she were buzzed, her voice all heady with desire as she rubbed the tip of his cock against her lips. Heat blasted through his body as he watched her sinful mouth caress his erection, her tongue darting out to lick and kiss him. "Just like I've imagined."

"You've imagined this?" he rasped out, but she could only nod an answer because she'd stopped teasing now, and she was swirling her tongue up and down his shaft. He couldn't see straight. He couldn't think straight. Hell, he didn't want to think ever again. He only wanted this. Her mouth was warm and wet and soft, and her hands were quick and nimble, and all the sensations at once threatened to annihilate him.

And that's exactly what he wanted. He wanted to be lost in her, lost in pleasure, lost in feelings. He threaded his fingers farther into her hair, pulling her close.

"You look so hot, and you feel so fucking good, I can

barely take it," he groaned, gripping her head harder, as if he had to hold on to her.

She made some kind of moaning sound as her tongue worked him over. She grabbed tight at the base of his shaft with her hand, and the twin sensations did him in. His spine crackled, and he could feel the build starting. He leaned his head back, curse words falling from his mouth with abandon as her lips raced up and down his cock.

She was killing him, and he wanted it, he wanted to be obliterated by this, to be undone by her as he started to come, his half-formed words making her grip him even tighter with those perfect fucking lips. She kept going, licking and sucking until there was nothing left, and he was spent. Wrung dry, and he felt like he could sleep peacefully for days now with the kind of voodoo magic her lips had worked on him.

He knelt down with her, giving her a sweet, hot kiss on the forehead. He pulled up his boxers and jeans, then wrapped her into his arms and declared, "Now I can die a happy man."

"Don't die," she said, and there was real fear in her voice. She wasn't playing around.

"I won't. I promise," he said, and it felt true. Everything with her felt true, especially the rapid beat of her heart. He could feel it against his chest.

"You can't promise that," she whispered in a thin voice.

"I know. But I want to," he said, wrapping his arms tightly around her, holding her there on the floor of his bar where no one could see them. Then he gently placed a hand on her chin, making her look at him. Her brown eyes were so pure and deep, but there was so much sadness in them. "When you told me you're not in the place for a relationship. Was that the truth?"

"Yes. And no," she said, and he could tell it was hard for her to admit that much.

"Yes, you're not in the place for a relationship? Or not with me?" He motioned from her to him.

"You said the same thing about yourself," she pointed out, her tone edging toward defensive.

"I know," he whispered, then leaned in to kiss her forehead again, then her cheek, then her lips, giving the softest kiss he'd ever given her. "But things changed."

She laughed. "Because of that super-awesome, amazing blow job I gave you?"

He laughed, too, but then let it fade. He needed to make it clear to her that this wasn't because she'd given him the blow job of a lifetime. He was going to have to make it patently clear that there was so much more going on than the way their bodies collided into each other like magnets. He hadn't reached out to her today as he'd promised, because he'd spent the time thinking about how it would feel not to see her again. The answer was simple—awful. And now it was time to let her know.

"No. Because of how I feel when I'm with you."

She drew in a quick breath. "How do you feel when you're with me?"

Now it was his turn to inhale, steeling himself for what he was going to say. "Like I'm living in the present. Not the past." The admission didn't hurt as much as he'd thought it would. It felt freeing.

She placed a gentle hand over his cheek. He closed his eyes briefly, then opened them. "Can you tell me what happened in Chicago? Because I think it's a big part of what's going on in here," she said, tracing a line across his forehead.

He felt a stabbing pain in his chest, as if his organs were constricting and seizing up, but when she ran her hand over his jawline, the soft pads of her fingers tracing him, that tightening went away.

He pushed his hand through his hair. "You know when you asked me about the family here? The kids and that fire a few weeks back?"

She nodded, listening intently.

"The reason I didn't want to talk about it is because of why I came here in the first place. I love it here now, and that's partly because it's everything Chicago wasn't for me anymore. Because everywhere I went I couldn't escape the memories of this one fire where I lost two of my men," he said, and his voice threatened to break, and hell, he didn't want to lose it in front of her or anyone. But then she reached for his hand, squeezing tight, and that gave him the strength to keep going, to tell her the full story.

"It was a cold night in February. Someone left candles in a condo when they went out to the movies. It was one of those things—you're rushing to leave, to make it to the theater in time, and you forget. Ladder 10 got the call when it started, and the fire was raging in minutes. Pretty soon, the whole top floor was consumed," he said, steeling himself as the images threatened to choke him.

"I was on one of the lower floors with the chief and my buddy Sawyer, fighting the blaze. We did everything right. Did it by the books. We were safe, we took precautions, and we were just trying to fight the beast. Then a wall collapsed." He lowered his hand sharply, like a drawbridge closing, to demonstrate the speed. "The chief saw it coming. As soon as it started to fall, he pushed Sawyer and me to try to get us out of the way," he said, giving voice for the first time to the reel that played behind his eyes. The story hurt in the way that thick sobs do when you try to hold back, but not quite in the suffocating way it had felt inside his head all these days. Maybe just telling it was what he'd needed, coupled with the caring way Megan watched and listened as he spoke.

"I was the *lucky* one," he said with a small scoff. "Or so they all said after, because all I suffered were shoulder injuries. Trust me, I sure as hell didn't think about how much my body ached at the funeral a few days later when the chief and Sawyer were laid to rest. All I thought about was what happened. Sometimes it's still all I think about. I replay it, I study it. I try to figure out if there was something, *anything*, I could have done differently. I tried to tell myself that Sawyer's death was the equivalent of a friend being hit in the crosswalk by a car that ran the light."

"It was the same," she said, threading her fingers more tightly through his. Her touch warmed him all over, loosening another layer of pain he'd wrapped himself in.

He shrugged helplessly. "Maybe I could have grabbed Sawyer harder when the wall was falling. I don't know, Megan," he said, looking her in the eyes. Hers were rimmed with sadness, like his, he was sure. Only there was a certainty in her gaze that he didn't possess, but wanted to. "I don't know anymore. I will never know." He stopped and took a deep breath. "So that's what happened in Chicago."

He'd done it. He'd told the story he rarely told. He'd managed to get through it without his chest caving in or his soul dying a little more. He'd survived once more.

Now that he was finished, she petted his hair with her

other hand, and he was dangerously close to letting go of all the walls he'd built up, because of this. Because of her, nestled in the corner of his bar with him, in this small town that had somehow become his new home. Listening, touching, soothing.

"And you feel guilty because you're alive," she said softly.

He nodded, looking at his hands as he talked. "And because I didn't save them."

"But you couldn't," she said, in a strong, clear voice. "Because there was nothing you could have done differently. You did everything you could. You were safe, you took precautions, you did your job, and even so it still happened."

He looked up at her, her hands still running through his hair. He didn't want her to stop touching his hair. It felt too good, especially now, especially with this.

"There was *nothing* you could have done differently. Things just happen," she said again. "It's the risk you take in your job. It's the chance you take. That sometimes you save, and sometimes you don't. But a wall comes crumbling down in a five-alarm fire, and you're lucky to be alive, Becker. That's all that separates you from Sawyer and the chief. It's not anything more than luck. It could just as easily have been Sawyer standing where you were. But it wasn't, and for no reason other than luck. It's not anyone's fault that you're still standing and they're not. It's random. It's chaos. It's the absolute unpredictability of life and circumstances and fate."

She was so certain in her words, but so caring, and it was as if a rigid piece of his heart cracked a tiny bit, and in that space, he wanted to let her all the way in. "How can you be so wise? Because of your dad?"

She swallowed and nodded. Her eyes were wide and

edged with tears, but her voice cut through the sadness. "I never even knew him. And it sucked, but I had no choice except to figure things out and keep on moving. Keep on living. My mom wasn't the same then, Becker. She was a wreck, and Travis and I had to learn to make it through the day all on our own. That's why we're so close."

"Do you miss your dad?"

"I miss the idea of him. But I also feel like he's with me, the best parts of him," she said, rubbing her hand against her tattoo.

His heart lurched toward her, and he immediately pressed his lips against her shoulder, lightly dusting her ink, then looked at her. "You're probably going to think I'm crazy, but I saw an owl a few nights ago when I couldn't sleep."

She furrowed her brow at him. "Where was the owl?"

"On a branch in a tree in the backyard. I looked out the kitchen window and there it was. I don't know why. And maybe this is crazy, but it made me think of you. But then, I was already thinking of you."

"It's the same for me. About you."

"I haven't been able to stop thinking about you, Megan. Not since that first night you came back to my house. Not since that time at the station. Not since we ran together. Not since you painted your body. Not since you walked into my life and showed up on the back porch of my bar. I can't get you out of my head, and you're the only thing that makes me feel like a fucking human being again, and not like some ghost stuck in the past."

"The damage you've seen doesn't have to define you, Becker," she said, and he dipped his forehead to hers.

"I could say the same about you. Because I think that's

the real reason you don't want to pursue anything serious with me. It's not because of your brother. And it's not because of your ex. It's not even because you're leaving town. It's because of what I do, isn't it?"

"I've always had a terrible fear of bar owners," she teased.

"Yeah, I thought so."

Then she turned serious, and whispered, "I don't want anything to happen to you. I don't want to get close to you and then lose you."

Her voice was haunted and full of so much pain, but longing, too. He felt that longing and didn't want to fight it. He only wanted to give in to it. To her. To how he felt with her. Her touch was some kind of magic. The way she talked to him like a massage. He was finally starting to say goodbye to the twisted, torn-up way he replayed and rewound and revisited his past, and it was because of her. Here, nestled together, he was keenly aware that she was the start of something. He didn't want to wait any longer for her. He didn't want to hold back any more.

"I don't want to get lost. Except in you. I want to know you, Megan. I want to have more nights like this. Even if our time is limited, even though you're leaving for Portland in a week, I want as much of you as I can have right now. I hope to God you want the same."

• • •

When he said things like that, she felt stripped bare. As if her heart were beating outside her body. It scared the living daylights out of her, but she was so drawn to him, like he was air or breath. She couldn't deny she wanted the same thing.

She didn't know how to reconcile these opposing forces in her—self-preservation versus taking a leap. But maybe he was right. You only live once, and anything can happen to anyone. Hell, she'd chosen a safe man before—an internet start-up guy—and look where that had landed. Then, if a guy like Craig—who had the safest job in the world selling books to happy people in a tourist town—could break his leg trying to save a kid and almost die, did her rules even apply? Maybe they'd been useful at one point, but perhaps she'd outrun them.

Maybe she'd been holding on to her fears when she'd actually outgrown them a while ago. She'd survived the loss of her father, she'd handled her mom's depression, she'd extricated herself from a damaging relationship before it went too far. She'd moved on and through and past, and here she was on the other side.

There were a million ways to lose someone, and sometimes you lost them before they even left this earth. It was time to move on. To split from her past. To step forward, even in this small way, for this brief moment in time.

"Me, too," she said, surprised at the strength of her declaration. "Where do we go from here? I'm only here for another week. I want the same thing, but I'm leaving soon."

"We make the most of the time you have. It's as simple as that. But we need to do right by Travis going forward. I'm seeing him at the firehouse tomorrow morning. We need to tell him. I need to be the one to do it, okay?"

She nodded. She understood the man code. She knew how these firefighters were and that wanting to date someone's sister had to be discussed man-to-man first. "He's in Monterey for that executive game and coming back late tonight. We have one of the final shoots for the calendar to-morrow morning."

"I'll talk to him then."

She nodded, but nerves whisked through her. She fidg-eted with the bracelet on her wrist, and that caught his atten-tion. He gently lifted her chin so she was facing him.

"Hey," he said softly, brushing his thumb along her jaw. "You worried about what he'll say?"

"I just don't want to let him down when he finds out I lied to him."

Becker's eyes were somber as he nodded. "I know what you mean. Trust me, I know what you mean. But I'm just going to tell him that this is real. This thing between you and me."

"It is real," she said insistently, placing her hand on top of his. The clock was ticking loudly; time was winding down, marching to the end of her stay here. Whatever was happen-ing between them felt like falling for a city when you're on a vacation. Wonderful, but short-lived, with the ending in sight before they began. "And since it is, we should make the most of it while I'm here," she said, trying to keep the sadness that would come with good-bye far away from them.

"We should," he said quietly as he reached for her hand. "And who knows what's next. You're leaving, and I can't make promises, but no matter how hard we try we can't stay away. So let's see what happens while you're here, and we'll deal with you leaving when it gets here."

She nodded crisply. That sounded realistic, and possible.

He leaned in to dust a soft kiss on her forehead, her nose, ever so briefly on her lips. "And now, I'd really like to spend this time you have in town with you instead of resisting you," he said, and threaded his fingers through her hair. She shivered at his touch, sparks skipping over her skin at his words. "I want to take you out to dinner, and get to know you even better, and I want to hold your hand, and kiss you across the table, before I take you back to my house and get reacquainted with your exquisite body."

"Becker." She shuddered, desperate for him to touch her. "I can barely think when you talk like that."

"Good. I don't want you thinking. I want you feeling, because if you're thinking then I'm not doing it right."

He reached for her hand and lifted her to her feet.

"Hey. Do you remember when we first met and how you wanted me to draw a raccoon?" she asked.

"No, Megan. I forgot everything about the night I met the woman who makes me feel human again," he said in a dry voice.

She rolled her eyes. "Oh, ha ha." She reached into her purse for her sketchbook and flipped to the page with the raccoon she'd drawn for him. The tattoo she'd told him about by the river. She held her breath as he appraised the image, so different from the silly one she'd drawn that first night, but similar in many ways, too. The raccoon was painstakingly detailed, down to the tufts of fur on his ringed tail, but he had the cartoonish look that marked her favorite style. The best part was how she'd dressed him. She'd given him a pair of bunker pants, suspenders, and a fire helmet. Her skin prickled with anxiety, hoping he liked it.

He looked at her, ran a thumb along her jawline, and held her face in his hands. "You drew me a raccoon."

She nodded.

"I love it."

"You do?"

"You're good, Megan. You're really good. You're going to be an amazing tattoo artist. You have so much talent."

She ripped the page out. "I want you to keep it," she said softly, her chest flooding briefly with nerves. She liked giving her drawings away; she'd always made pictures for other people, and she had for him their first night together, so it seemed fitting. Grabbing a pen from her purse, she whipped off a few quick lines, then handed him the paper.

With his eyes on the page, he read her words out loud. "For you. Some people might think a drawing of a raccoon is silly. I'm one of those people. I'm also not. I'm glad you're both too. Megan." He looked up from the lines and brushed his index finger gently along her cheek. "I already loved it. Now I love it even more. And I'm going to add it to my Megan collection."

"You have a collection for me?"

"You did leave me a note that first night," he pointed out.

"Now you have another."

"That I do. And I love that you draw pictures and leave notes for me. It's part of what makes you unbelievably hot to me," he said. He made a noise that bordered on a growl and pulled her in for a hungry, desperate kiss. Soon, they were tangled up in each other, and she was groaning at the feel of his chest against her. He grabbed her at the waist, and she wrapped her legs around him as he lifted her onto the counter and kissed her furiously, his bristly jawline turning her cheeks red. She didn't care one bit that she was getting whisker burn.

Finally, he broke the kiss.

She placed a hand on her chest. "I want to do something."

He arched an eyebrow.

"Meet me on the back porch."

The sliver of a smile played on his lips. "As you wish."

Pushing open the front door, she waved good-bye with a sexy wink, then walked quickly down the street, around the side of the building, and turned into the alley, lit faintly by a streetlamp that illuminated him. He stood in the doorway, waiting for her, a curious look on his face. As she neared the table where she'd taken that tumble, she started to reach under her skirt.

When it registered, he grinned wildly. That first night she'd promised she'd show up again in the alley and shimmy out of her panties. She walked around the table, stopped inches from him and skimmed off her undies, handing the little scrap of pink lace to him. "I told you I'd give them to you," she whispered.

He brought them to his nose briefly, then stuffed them into his pocket as he tugged her against him. "And I told you I'd make you come again."

She tapped her finger playfully against her chin, as if she were recalling the fine details of their naughty conversation. "Why, I believe you did."

He scanned the alley. It was as quiet as the night they met. The only soundtrack was the faint rustle of a night breeze in the nearby trees, and the faraway music from the Kings of Leon album playing on repeat from inside the Panting Dog.

"Let's make the most of our week then," he said as he clasped her hand and dropped into a chair a few feet away, pulling her into his lap. He reached into his back pocket and brandished a condom.

"Excellent. Because I'm already good to go," she said,

since she was amped up from their kisses, and their contact behind the bar. She made quick work of his zipper and yanked his briefs down, freeing his erection. Gripping him in her hand once more, she savored his reaction as he groaned hungrily from her touch, his eyes floating closed as she covered him. Hot sparks spread throughout her body as she hiked up her skirt and lowered herself, inch by fantastic inch, until he filled her completely. She gripped his shoulders as she began to move, upping the pace.

Grasping her hips, he held on to her, letting her set the tempo. "Like that?" he asked, as he lowered his mouth to her neck, kissing a path down her skin to the hollow of her throat.

"Yes. Just like that," she said in broken breaths as they kept up for several hot and heady minutes. She loved that he was such an attentive lover, wanting to know what pleased her, what thrilled her, and what made her shatter.

The answers were all one and the same. *Him.*

Soon, she wrapped her arms around his neck, letting her head fall onto his shoulder as the pleasure intensified, sweeping through her body like a rainstorm bursting from the sky. "You're so good to me," she moaned, concentrating on the climax that was rising up to greet her. He gripped her hips, quickly taking the reins, guiding her moves as he drove her over the edge, her body bathed in the bliss of their coming together.

Minutes later, he layered kisses on her neck and whispered in her ear, "This is now my favorite image of Hidden Oaks. You, here on the back porch. With me."

She could hear in his voice the smile she was sure he was wearing.

Chapter Seventeen

Neither Becker nor Travis was on duty, but they were both at the firehouse for one of the final shoots. Becker as the captain, and Travis because, well, because he was a ham. But the photographer hadn't arrived yet, so Becker pulled his friend aside. He wasn't going to hem or haw, or let this gnaw away at him anymore. He didn't know how Travis was going to handle this, and he didn't know if this was the end to a friendship. But he knew this much—telling the truth was much better than the alternative. It was the only option.

"Hey, man. I need to talk to you."

Travis nodded, a serious expression on his face. He probably figured it was about work. They walked outside the firehouse and stood by the open garage.

Becker steeled himself for an unhappy reaction, but he didn't mince words. "Trav, I know you asked me not to get involved with your sister, but I wanted to let you know that I'm planning on taking her out tonight. On a date. Hoping that'll be all right by you."

Travis narrowed his eyebrows and tilted his head, as if he hadn't heard correctly. He didn't speak, just gave him a curious look. Becker had been expecting some huffing and puffing. Some lecture. Some man-to-man, don't-you-ever-hurt-my-sister kind of talk. Not this stony silence.

Travis scratched his ear. "What? What did you say?"

"I'm going out with Megan. Tomorrow night," he repeated.

Travis breathed out hard. Shook his head. "What the fuck?"

"She's a grown woman. She can date who she wants."

"Yeah, I know *that*. But I told you to stay away from her..." He let his voice trail off, then held his hands out wide. "You know how I feel about this."

"I know. I know, man. You did, and I didn't listen to you. And for that I am sorry. But the truth is I met her the night before I knew it was her, and we connected, and there's just something there we want to explore."

Travis cringed. His features contorted; his eyebrows nearly twisted. "You *connected*? What the hell?"

Becker nodded, keeping his voice steady and even. "We did, and we've spent time together on the shoot, and working on the calendar. And I know you said you don't want me involved with her, but we feel something for each other. Something real."

Travis kept shaking his head, as if he could rid himself of what Becker was saying. "I thought you were against relationships. I thought you didn't even believe in them." Travis slashed his hand through the air. "*Never*, you said. It only leads to trouble. And with my sister of all people? I love her like crazy, man. Do you have any idea what she means to me? Do you have any clue? Growing up, we had nothing but each other."

"I do have an idea. I have a brother. I know what it's like to care about someone, Trav."

"She deserves the world, man. And you're still stuck in Chicago."

The words cut him to the quick. They sliced through him cruelly with the truth, and he swore for a second he could feel the pain as if he'd truly been cut. But then the feeling drifted away, like it had with Megan. Maybe he was moving on. Maybe he was finally starting to heal.

"I was," he said in a low voice. "But I'm starting not to be, and it feels good."

Travis narrowed his eyes, like he didn't believe him. "So that's it? You just changed?"

Was it that simple? Hell, maybe that was it. "Yeah, things changed. I met your sister. And I'm crazy about her."

Travis scoffed. "You telling me you've been involved with her already?"

Becker swallowed a thick knot. "Yes."

Travis cursed, then let out a long stream of air. "You lied to me, man. That is not cool."

"I know. And I hope you'll forgive me for it."

"So you've been messing around with her the whole time she's been in town?"

"Look, we met the first night," he said, shoving a hand roughly through his hair. "I didn't know she was your sister, and we agreed to stay away from each other after we realized. But that didn't happen, and I'm sorry, but I'm not sorry as well," he added, standing his ground.

"Are you just fucking her?" he asked, and it sounded like

a vile accusation, one Becker had to defuse.

"Travis. Listen to me. I know I lied to you when I said nothing had happened. And I'm sorry. But get this through your head. I'm fucking crazy about her, and the last thing I want to do is hurt her. I swear. I know things about her. I know that Mud Pie Brownies are her favorite, and she made them with you and sold them in the town square when you were kids. And you also taught her to make a dam, and spent endless hours with her by the river when you were kids. I also know that she's afraid of losing the people she loves. She's afraid of losing you, but somehow she's managed to live with that, too. And I know she's an amazing cartoonist and draws these incredible pictures of silly animals, and I know she's smart and funny and sarcastic and vulnerable as hell. And that she cares so deeply about you and what you think of her, and she hates the thought of letting you down, because she looks up to you so damn much."

Travis was silent for several seconds. "Damn," he said, finally speaking as he chased that word with a low whistle of admiration.

Becker continued. "So we can do this the easy way. Or we can do it the hard way. But either way, I'm taking her out, and I'd much rather do it with your blessing."

Travis shook his head several times. The look on his face bordered on resignation, but not acceptance.

"I can't do that yet. I just can't. You just dropped this on me, and I can't stand here and say I'm okay with it. I won't plaster on a happy face because you say you're all fixed up now," he said, tapping the side of his head. "But I get it. You're doing it regardless, and the two of you are adults, so this is your choice. Just remember this, if you hurt her…"

He didn't finish his sentence, but he didn't need to. Becker understood he'd be dead to him if he did wrong by Megan.

. . .

It was a scene that could cause rubbernecking for miles.

Megan thanked her lucky stars that she knew how to shoot a picture. Because it didn't get much better than this. Today was the requisite beefcake shot—the necessary photo of the guys washing the truck. Funny thing was, the setup wasn't just calendar man-candy. The firefighters really did wash the trucks every day. With schoolkids coming by to visit the firehouse, as well as citizens popping in when they wanted to, the engines acquired fingerprints and dirt quickly. The men kept the engines spit-shined and polished since they were always, effectively, on display.

Jackson looked mighty fine soaping up the door, dressed only in his navy-blue pants and work boots, his chiseled abs on display and his wavy dark hair wet at the tips. He'd make quite the fantasy man for some woman someday, Megan mused as she shot more pics. Smith, naturally, ably filled the part, too, as he sprayed the hose over the tires. Megan snapped a few extra close-ups just for Jamie, who'd probably squeal when she saw them. Even though Jamie got to partake of the real thing, she was proud of her man's role in the calendar, and the fact that he'd likely grace the cover again.

There were other guys, too, and as Megan captured more action shots of the men at work, including her brother, she had a hunch that this calendar would be enjoyed. Her work on the shoot was almost done. She'd snagged most of the solo shots she needed, as well as the group pics of the guys, including one of four of the men silhouetted against a dark sky, helmets low on their foreheads, heavy tools in their hands. Pure dark smolder and enough variety in the size and shape of the men to please most red-blooded women. That Becker was one of the guys in that shot didn't inform her unbiased, professional opinion at all. At least, that's what she told herself. Though as soon as the thought had flickered into her brain, igniting a private little grin, she knew she was a goner.

Something had changed last night. Shifted. They'd admitted their fears and decided to give things a shot, even just for a week. Would that make it harder for her to leave for Portland? Already, she cared deeply for him, more than she'd ever expected to. Was she opening herself up to the possibility of a whole new level of heartache when she hit the road in seven days?

She pictured the week unspooling in days and nights of bliss, and then slamming cruelly into the finish line in only one week. That end was bound to hurt in a new fresh way.

A knot of worry crept through her from all the unknown.

Then she felt a tingling in her spine. She didn't dare look away from the viewfinder because she was ringing up some damn fine shots. But she *knew* he'd just walked past her. He hadn't even touched her. He hadn't even lazily traced a finger across her back. Instead, she could simply sense the shape of him; she could smell the clean, sexy scent of him; she could simply *feel* the way he was near her.

"Can't wait to see you later."

The words were the barest of a whisper on her neck. They sent a rush of heat down through her veins, and goose bumps erupted over her skin. A proper date. Not just a stolen moment in the bar, in his house, by the river.

Later, as she finished the shoot and started to pack up her gear, she felt a familiar pair of arms wrap around her shoulders. Then knuckles dig into her skull. "You didn't think I'd stop giving you noogies just because you've basically ignored every single thing I told you to do?"

She shifted around. "Nice to see you, too."

"Listen," he said, his tone shifting to serious. "I only worry about you because I love you. Because I can't stop looking out for you. And because I want you to have the world."

"I know," she said softly.

"I'm not happy about this, but I can't stop you, so just know that I'm here for you no matter what happens, okay?"

Her throat hitched, but she held it together. This was her brother. This was the man she looked up to, admired, trusted. He would always be there for her, no matter what. She was lucky to have had him growing up, and she was luckier to have him now.

He lowered his voice. "I love you, Megan."

"I love you, Trav."

Chapter Eighteen

Decked out in jeans, red boots, and a silvery shirt that seemed like it was having a mighty fine time hugging her breasts, Megan looked edible to him.

She also looked enrapt, and that made him so damn happy.

Her brown eyes were wide and sparkling as she took in the exhibit at the art gallery in a nearby town. His brother, the *sensitive, artistic* one, had suggested he take her here. He'd emailed Griffin and asked for a recommendation, and immediately he'd sent back the info. *If I were in Northern California like you, you'd have to tear me away from an exhibit of cartoon art*, his younger brother had written.

That was all he'd needed to hear. Griffin and Megan had similar tastes and interests in art as far as Becker, with his untrained eye, could tell. Judging from the way Megan studied every illustration in the room, as if she were memorizing all the lines, curves, and colors, she couldn't be happier. That reaction to him was priceless. In their short time together—albeit sneaking around—she'd already done so much for him. He'd wanted to be able to do something special for her, to show her that there was more to the two of them than the intense physical connection.

She reached for his hand and laced her fingers through his, and her touch warmed his very soul. "I think I'm in love with this exhibit," she said as she looked at him.

"That makes me happy," he said.

Being able to show her something she loved made his heart feel full. It was a foreign feeling to him, and it almost seemed as if he were wearing a pair of shoes that were a bit too tight, or a bit too loose. But his heart didn't hurt, and it wasn't painful; it would simply take some adjusting.

"Thank you for finding this for me."

"Griffin gets all the credit. I'm just glad you like it."

As they walked to the next work, a slinky woman in a dress wearing a floppy hat, her eyes lit up once more. "That," she said, pointing in a frenzy as she dropped his hand. "Can't you just see me inking that on some big burly man's shoulder or something?"

He couldn't quite see it for a guy, but he wasn't one to knock down her dreams. "The woman with the hat?"

She laughed and shook her head. "No. The hat. Look at what's on the hat."

He peered closer, spotting a streak of silhouetted birds, flying across the brim. Simple, sleek, and yet powerful. "That I could definitely see," he said, then turned to her, enjoying the mesmerized look in her eyes. "Look at you, finding inspiration here. Maybe you don't need to go to Portland," he said, then he stopped speaking abruptly, the weight of his unexpected statement hitting him hard in the gut. He gulped and stepped back. He hadn't planned to suggest that; he wasn't even sure where the notion came from…except maybe from deep inside him. From his hope to know her more, and better. From a wish to have this woman in his life on more than just a temporary basis. For her to stay. But he didn't want to quash her dreams. He wasn't going to be that guy.

The gallery was harshly silent for a moment, and it was as if this connection between the two of them revolved around this moment. Because one week hardly seemed sufficient anymore. That he would miss her was more than apparent. That he wanted more of her was patently obvious to him now. "Or maybe when you go, you can come back from time to time," he offered, his heart beating far too fast.

She closed the distance between them, placing her hand on his chest. "Maybe I can. Maybe I would like that."

He let out a breath he barely realized he was holding. "Maybe I would like that, too," he whispered, and he liked that they were saying *maybe*. It was a hopeful maybe; it was the suggestion of a promise, the possibility of more.

He looped his hand around her tiny waist, curving his arm around her body. She trembled under his touch. His blood heated at the way she responded, and he was tempted to press her up against the stark white wall of this gallery, between the woman in the hat and the inked drawing of a skyscraper next to her, and kiss her so hard she'd forget her name.

Drag his mouth across her skin. Hear her whimper.

"Maybe we need to get out of here right now," she suggested.

"It's like you can read my mind."

"Or your body," she said, wiggling her eyebrows, and damn, if he wasn't already hooked, she had reeled him all the way in tonight. Her easy way with him, with words and with laughter, made him want her more.

"I need to be with you," he said, his voice a rough scrape. "Come over. Spend the night with me. Let me make you breakfast in the morning. I'm off tomorrow. We can go for a run or make Mud Pie Brownies or whatever you want."

She parted her lips, breathed out, heat practically radiating in waves off her body. Her eyes were hazy with lust, but she managed a playful tease. "Becker, I'm gonna be blunt here. I sort of figured that's the way the evening was going. Especially since my mom's back in town, so I think your house is better than mine."

Holding hands, they left the gallery and headed to his truck. He opened the passenger door and let her in, memorizing every move of her beautiful body as she buckled into the front seat. He walked around and got in his side.

"You look mighty hot on your bike, Megan. But you look even better in something a little safer."

"Like your truck?"

"My truck. A car. Anything other than a bike."

"You trying to tell me you don't want me riding a bike?"

"If I had any say in the matter, that's what I'd be saying."

"Well, I don't see myself abandoning my bike anytime soon, just like I don't see you abandoning your job anytime soon, so maybe we should just call that one a draw," she said.

"Touché."

"But you do like the way I look in your truck, you were saying?" she said in a purr, as she dragged her hand along her thigh. He hitched in a breath.

"Now you're not playing fair," he said as he turned on the ignition and backed up.

"I know," she murmured as she played with the button on her jeans, teasing him with the possibility of her undressing.

"I take it you want me to be able to drive."

She nodded. "I do. I want to be at your house."

The image of her spread out on his bed occupied every single thought he had as he drove to Hidden Oaks, his arms gripping the wheel tight because if they didn't, then he'd be all over her. He could smell her in the enclosed space—the dizzying smell of that vanilla-sugar lotion she wore—and it made his mouth water for her. He'd already undressed her in his mind and was running his hands over her soft skin, his lips, his tongue, nipping at her, nibbling at that tantalizing flesh where her thighs met her backside. That delicious little line…

She squeezed his thigh as he drove, and leaned in to plant hot kisses on his neck.

"You're making it hard to concentrate on the road," he said.

She palmed his erection through his jeans. He wanted to grab her hand and press down hard against his dick. "Hard is sort of the plan," she said.

He slowed at a light and turned to look at her. Her eyes were wild and playful. He moved in for a kiss, and he could feel her breath soft against his lips. But he pulled back when he was millimeters away, to give her a taste of her own teasing medicine. "You sure you don't want me to take you home and give you a kiss good-night on the porch? Be a gentleman and all?" he asked as the light turned green and he continued down the road.

She rubbed him through the fabric of his pants. "You better be taking me to your home tonight," she said, then paused deliberately and unzipped her jeans some, her fingertips dancing perilously close to where he wanted to be tonight.

He inhaled sharply as he turned onto his road. "Megan," he said, his voice a warning. "When you play dirty, I'm going to have to punish you."

"How are you going to punish me?"

"I'm going to tease the living fuck out of you until you're begging me to make you come."

Now it was her turn to shudder. Judging from the way her chest rose and fell, she was as enticed by the idea as he was.

Soon, they reached his house, and he parked next to her bike that she'd ridden over earlier. After turning off the engine, he reached for the car door but didn't make it. In a second, she unbuckled and launched herself onto him, tangling her arms around him, capturing his mouth in hers, like a tiger diving in for a feast. He groaned and responded instantly, drawing her tongue deeper into his mouth, devouring her taste, her lips.

She was heady, and every single thing about her lit up all his senses, including the intoxicating scent that made him want to run his tongue all over her body, from her ankle, up her legs, across her belly and her breasts, and then between her legs. He broke the kiss and she whimpered at the lack of contact, but then he bent his head to her neck and inhaled her. "You smell so fucking good," he said, and licked her from her earlobe down the column of her throat.

She moaned his name, and his cock strained against his

jeans to hear her say that like he was the answer to all the fevered questions her body was asking.

"Inside," he growled. "Now."

Once inside his house, he watched her walk up the stairs, remembering the last time she was here. If he'd known who she was that first night, he'd never have taken her home. Thank God for anonymity. Not knowing was the best thing that happened to him, because it gave him the chance to be with her. Now, they had all night and all day tomorrow, too. But not much more. She'd be leaving soon. Too soon. Already, he wasn't sure that he'd be able to say good-bye so easily. Or at all. For now, she was here. She was his, and he was going to take what he could get and savor it.

She walked into his bedroom and turned around, her dark eyes saying everything.

She raised her arms, and in seconds he was inches away, peeling off her shirt. He pulled back to enjoy the view, drawing in a sharp breath. She was beautiful. Strong arms, soft curves, and a flat belly that begged to be kissed. She wore a pink-and-white-striped bra that made him think of a candy cane, and then that made him think of nothing but what lay beneath that lace, so he unhooked the bra with one swift flick. The fabric fell to her shoulders and revealed her round, full breasts with dark pink nipples. He kissed one breast, tugging with his tongue and lips, as he cupped the other one, kneading her soft, supple flesh. She pulled him down onto his bed, wriggling under him, moans and whimpers falling from her lips.

He could have spent all night on her breasts, but her belly was too inviting, so he rained kisses from the top of her ribs to the open zipper on her jeans. He could feel the heat from between her legs.

"Take my clothes off. Please." Her voice was raspy, full of heat and need, and the sound made his head cloudy.

"Are you sure?"

"Undress me now," she said, and her voice was practically a pant.

"If you insist."

She pushed off her boots as he tugged her jeans down over her hips, his breath hitching at the sight of her nearly naked body once more. She wore matching striped panties that were so tiny they barely covered her. She kicked off her jeans as he slid a hand between her legs. Her panties were soaked, and he loved being able to feel her wetness all the way through the fabric. He lowered his head to her, inhaling her scent, and his raging hard-on was like steel now, knocking to be freed.

"I'm so turned on, I'll probably come the second you touch me," she said.

The idea of that thrilled him. "And you used to be the marathoner."

"Not with you. You know how to do everything to me to make me lose my mind," she said. Her voice was all ragged, and she sounded both vulnerable and crazy turned on. She wanted him to fuck her and make love to her at the same time—his kind of woman.

"Good. I like the way you are with me. Only with me," he said, running his hands along her thighs and spreading her legs.

"I want you so much. I need you now." The look on her face was so sexy, and so desperate, and he could barely believe he'd done this to her. That she was giving herself to him so fully, with abandon, with a dark and desperate need.

"If you were any sexier, it'd be a crime," he said, as he settled between her legs, pulled her panties to the side and licked her once, his tongue drawing a line across her delicious pussy.

She gasped, and her voice rose an octave. He looked up at her. "Hmm. I must not be doing it right."

"Please, Becker. Touch me again."

He looped a finger through the panel of her panties, swept her again, stopping briefly to flick her clit with the tip of his tongue. Another high-pitched moan fell on his ears as she rocked her hips into his face. He pulled back, giving her another playful look. "Hmm. You're not there yet. What are we going to do about you?"

She grabbed at his hair, trying to return him to the promised land.

"No. I want you another way."

"Anything. Anything you want."

He moved up so he could kiss her mouth, and she grabbed hungrily at him as he tugged off her panties, leaving her naked and perfect beneath him. With his hands gripping her waist, he shifted her around so she straddled him as he lay on his back. He lifted her by her hips, hovered her over his chest, watching her expression as her eyes went wide with desire. He lowered her over his face, holding her thighs gently but firmly as he rocked her against his lips.

Quickly, her breathing became heavier, and her pants turned into a random combination of *Oh God*s and his name, over and over, as he drank her in, his tongue racing across her decadent wetness, the taste of her on his lips. He watched her the whole while, her breasts bouncing as she rocked against his mouth, one hand pressed against her face as if the pleasure were too intense for her to bear.

His entire body felt alive and electric as he consumed her.

Eyes closed, lips parted, she leaned forward, bracing against the wall for balance. Soon her movements became erratic, and her mouth fell open in a perfect O as she moaned and gasped. He gripped her hips harder, wanting to drown in her. She was a sight to behold as she fucked his face, and he zeroed in on her. Harder, faster, more furious, until she shouted his name and bucked against his mouth, losing the last shred of control as she went over the edge.

He chased her with his tongue, savoring every delicious drop of her as the aftershocks spread through her body, and she shuddered several times but didn't move. Her hands were still locked to the wall, it seemed, and her body was angled over him, and he could barely breathe, but he didn't care, because he loved the fact that he'd just delivered a shattering orgasm to her, but yet it felt as if she'd fucked him like crazy.

Maybe she had. Soon, she let go of her grip on the wall, then sank to his side, wedging her naked body against his clothed one.

"Mmm," she said dreamily, her fingers fumbling at his shirt. "It's not fair that you have clothes on."

"So get me naked," he said.

She reached for his T-shirt, pulling it over his head. She stopped and drank him in with her eyes, her gaze setting his skin on fire as it roamed over his chest, his arms, his abs. Her hands fanned the flames as she skimmed them between his pecs, over his stomach, and down to his jeans. He toed off his shoes. She grappled with his belt buckle and jeans, letting them fall to the floor, then pushed his boxer briefs down too. He was completely aroused, aching for her touch.

Her eyes looked wild as her hand was drawn toward him. She wrapped her fingers around his cock and he shuddered. They were both so fevered.

"Condom," he rasped out, barely able to speak in sentences as she stroked his erection. "Nightstand."

The moment was eerily familiar, as if they'd fallen into déjà vu, but everything was different now. Because they were different. They were no longer two strangers tangling in the sheets in his home. They were two lovers who knew each other. They knew each other's fears, and hopes, and dreams. He wanted all of her, body and heart.

She scooted across the bed and reached for the foil packet. She opened it and rolled it on him. There was something intensely erotic about watching her cover him. Maybe it was because her hand was on him, maybe it was because her eyes were locked on his the whole time, or maybe it was just because it was the calm before the storm.

"Lie back," he instructed her, and she did, sliding up toward the pillows. She was so beautifully fucking inviting and ready for him. He bent down between her legs, groaning as he traced a finger against her. He held on to the base of his cock and teased her pussy with the tip, rubbing against her hot wetness. She gasped and her legs fell open easily. He pushed the head in, then looked in her eyes, staying completely still.

"Tell me what you want, Megan," he said.

She'd made it clear, but he wanted to hear it again and again.

"You," she said. "I want you."

"How do you want me?"

"I want you inside me," she said, and her voice was a wild plea, needy and hungry.

His hands pressed into the bed on each side of her, his cock barely in her. "Tell me how sure you are."

"I'm so sure. I want you so much. All of you," she said, and she looped her arms tightly around him, holding his ass, and trying to pull him in. "Make love to me now, Becker. "

Those were the magic words. He sank into her in one long, deep, driving thrust, and she made the sexiest sound when he filled her all the way up. She was so tight and her hot flesh surrounded him. She moved with him, slow and torturous strokes. She rocked her hips up, matching him thrust for thrust. He'd thought about this for days before last night outside his bar. He'd pictured another time with her, another chance in his bed, where he could have her the way he wanted. Now here he was, deep inside her, and she was wet and snug and gripping him hard. He reached for her leg, drawing it up over his shoulder.

"Oh God," she gasped.

"You like that? You like being so open for me?"

"Yes." She breathed out hard.

He draped her other leg over his shoulder, and now she was his, completely his, as he rocked deeper into her. With his weight resting on one arm, he ran his free hand down her body, from her neck to her breasts to her waist, the soft, teasing touch of his hand making her shiver, while the dizzying pace of his cock made her gasp relentlessly. She was losing herself to lust, to him, and he wanted her abandon. He drew a line across her belly, to the narrow space between their bodies, his finger sliding across her stomach, slick with perspiration.

Then he dropped his thumb down between her legs, rubbing her clit. She jammed her hands into his hair, grabbing at it, pulling him closer, forcing him to tuck his face into her neck. "Harder," she moaned, and he pressed his palms against the bed so he could surge into her, filling her to the hilt. She cried out, equal parts shock and savage pleasure as he slammed into her again and again, her voice rising, her cries a fevered pitch. She liked it hard, and she liked it when he was totally in control. He looked down at her, at the way she trembled, at how she bowed her back as he pumped deeper into her. She gripped his hair, fumbling for his mouth, grabbing at his lips with hers, her need for him rising into a frenzy.

"Tell me you're close," he whispered, his breath hot against her skin.

"So close."

He pumped into her at a frenetic pace, and she clenched around him, her thighs gripping him tighter. "I love the sounds you make, Megan. I love all your noises, your moans and cries." A bone-deep tingling shot through his spine. "I want to hear you come with me now." One more thrust did her in.

She shouted, and the sound of his name on her lips set him off. His climax tore through him, and he rode with her over the edge. She dragged her nails into his scalp, digging hard, and nothing else mattered in the whole universe except the absolute fucking heaven of coming with her.

She shuddered under him, and her legs fell off his shoulders. Soon, he collapsed onto her and she wrapped her arms around his back, her hands gently rubbing the sheen of sweat on him. She'd been a workout, all right. He'd never come so hard in his life.

"Be right back," he said and headed to the bathroom to take off the condom and toss it into the trash, then clean up. He returned to the bed and curled up next to her.

His heart still beat quickly, and he could feel hers too. He kissed her forehead, her cheek, then her lips, capturing her mouth with a long, slow, wet kiss that said as much about how he felt about her as the power of his orgasm.

When he broke the kiss, she looked at him, her brown eyes dreamy and pretty. He couldn't hold back anymore. He was in too deep. "I'm falling for you so fast, it's scary," he said.

The scary part was what would happen when she left town. That was the real fear now—he was finally letting go and feeling again, and she was going to walk out of his life.

Maybe. The word from the art gallery played in his head. Maybe they had a chance.

"I'm falling for you too," she said, tracing a soft line along his jaw.

More than a chance, he hoped.

"Let's keep falling together," he said. He brought her closer, holding her tight in his arms as they both drifted off to sleep.

Chapter Nineteen

"When do we get to the secret ingredient?"

Becker sounded disappointed, and Megan parked her hands on her hips. "Just you wait. We'll get there."

"I'm all for treats," he said, as he cracked an egg for the brownie mix on the kitchen counter the next morning. They'd already enjoyed eggs and toast and morning sex, and Becker had made a grocery store run while Megan had lounged on his couch, finishing the book she was reading on her phone as she waited for him. Funny, how she'd gone from self-protective and fearful, to ready or not in a matter of a few days. She hadn't shed all her worries in a week; that would be silly. But she was learning to live with them for the time being. She might still be scared, but she was dealing with it because the reward was worth it.

Now they were making her specialty. As she stirred the mix, he moved behind her, roped his arms around her waist and bent down to rain sweet, hot kisses on the back of her neck. She shivered under his touch and leaned her head back against his shoulder. "You do that and I won't be able to concentrate on these brownies."

"You in my shirt already makes me unable to concentrate," he growled, and inched his hand from her waist to the top button on his blue button-down that she'd commandeered from his closet this morning, searching for a fresh top to wear.

"Mmm…"

He unbuttoned one button on her shirt, dipping a hand inside to cup her breast, naked and uncovered. "You don't have a bra on."

"Why would I?"

"Good point. Just like the night I met you."

"You didn't even pretend that night that you looked away. You just watched me take it off, didn't you?"

"Of course I did. I wasn't going to miss a gorgeous woman stripping behind my bar. Besides, now I have you stripped in my house. Even better."

He feathered a calloused hand over her flesh, squeezing, then pinching her nipple as it hardened under his fingertips. She dropped the wooden spoon into the brownie bowl, closed her eyes, and pressed her back against his chest. Another button came undone, and soon the rest, then both of his hands were holding tight to her breasts, fondling them with the tantalizing mix of soft and rough that sent sparks of heat through her body and turned her panties wet. Good thing she'd tucked an extra pair in her purse before their date last night, so she had a fresh pair to pull on this morning.

"I'm going to need to keep extra undies here if you keep touching me like that." She wriggled her backside against him. At the first touch of his hard cock nestled against her rear, she moaned in satisfaction.

"Or just stop wearing underwear around me. Makes things easier," he said, in a hoarse voice. "Go commando on top. Go commando on bottom. Just be naked all the time."

"We'll never leave."

"Fine by me."

"Feel what you do to me, Becker." She grabbed his hand, guiding him between her legs. With one finger, he stroked the outside panel of the cotton panties that were already damp.

"There's nothing better than that," he whispered in her ear, his voice turning hazy. He ground against her backside, the steel length of him hard and heavy against her.

"I know of something better, and it involves you getting a condom right now."

He bit out a curse and gave her a quick slap on the butt. "Stay there. Don't move."

She didn't entirely follow his command. She stepped out of her undies, gripped the edge of the counter, and then flattened her back so she'd be in the perfect position when he returned.

He whistled under his breath. "That's a hell of a view."

She looked over her shoulder, a wicked grin on her face. He shook his head appreciatively, then gripped her ass with both hands, pressing into the soft flesh. He ran a thumb along the line where her cheeks met her thighs, then spread her wider.

"Damn, woman. I want to go down on you in this position."

She wouldn't have minded that any other time. But right now, she was aching between her legs. Wound tight with a throbbing need to feel him deep inside her.

"Just fuck me instead."

He skimmed down his jeans, rolled on a condom, and teased the head of his cock against her center.

"Have I told you how much I love being inside you?"

"Tell me again," she whispered.

"So unbelievably much."

"Then please take me now," she gasped.

"If you say so," he said, and in one hard thrust he filled her, and she released a breath she'd been holding. It was as if she'd been stunned, with shock and desire. In this position, she felt him even more deeply than the night before. He filled her all the way up, bordering on pleasure and pain with his size. She didn't want to move, because she teetered on that fine line. She tensed, and he bent over her, keeping still inside her. He moved her hair back gently, giving himself access to her neck. He kissed her tenderly behind her earlobe, then whispered to her, his hot breath causing goose bumps. "Relax, baby. I won't hurt you. I'll take it slow."

She nodded, breathed out, and let go of some of the tension she'd been holding on to in her belly. She sank deeper into a flat back, raised her ass higher, giving him more access, giving herself even less control. She liked letting go with him. Giving in to him. He could take her as much as he wanted to, because she wanted to be ravished.

She stretched her neck to look at him. "Do whatever you want to me," she whispered, and his eyes went hazy with lust.

She thought he would take her hard and fast. But he didn't. He moved slowly, as if he had all the time in the world. Each stroke was greeted with a moan, hot sparks shooting through her body. He moved in her like that, steady and luxurious. He was practically humming, enjoying the torture of the slow pace as he took his time, and kissed her neck, and made her moan nonstop. Her body was not her own. It was an instrument he played, like a virtuoso, and every move hit a new note of pleasure in her. She'd be singing an aria soon with the way he slid in and out. But she couldn't take the tease much longer. She wanted speed and friction now. She wanted to succumb to the ache between her legs.

"Becker," she cried out. "I can't take it anymore. It feels so fucking good, and I want more of you."

He needed no further instruction. He slammed into her. Hard, heavy, fast.

He grunted and pounded deeper, and each thrust sent her higher, and soon the world blurred, spiraling away as her orgasm descended on her, blasting through her, needing no assistance from his or her hand. She gasped sharply, barely managing words, hardly able to even say his name as she came on him. He chased her climax with his own, his large hands gripping her hips as he drove into her.

After he'd pulled out and cleaned up, she was still there, bent over, spent from the best hard fucking she'd ever experienced.

He kissed the small of her back, then ran his tongue along her spine and up to her neck, wrapping his hands around her waist to gently tug her away from the counter. He lifted her and carried her a few feet to a chair, letting her sink down on his lap.

"Did I turn you into a rag doll?"

"Yes," she whispered and looped her arms around his neck, finding his lips and kissing him tenderly. "But I'm glad."

"Me, too," he said, returning her kisses, his soft lips brushing against hers. "I hope you know I love kissing you as much as I love fucking you."

"I feel the same," she said, dropping her mouth to his one more time, claiming his lips with her own.

When she stopped, she tipped her forehead to the bowl they'd left on the counter. "Should we finish making the brownies?"

"Yeah, because I'm getting hungry from you making me service you all the time."

She raised an eyebrow. "Ha. I think you like my demands for your services."

He grabbed her hand. "I love your demands."

Megan retrieved her underwear from the floor and took off for the bathroom. After straightening up and washing her hands, she returned to the kitchen, and they finished mixing.

"And now for the secret ingredient," she said as she stirred.

"Dark chocolate. Like you told me at the river."

"You're a good listener," she said, then poured the batter into a baking pan.

Megan popped the mix into the oven, set the timer, and grabbed Becker's hand, leading him into the living room. She pulled him onto the couch with her, sliding alongside him.

She traced her finger across his lips. His eyes floated closed, and he sighed happily. She was going to miss him when she left for Portland. He'd mentioned last night that they might try to see each other still. Crazy thought, but then so was her being involved with him. Her stomach twisted with nerves, but she ignored the worry and charged forward. Making plans with Becker was not like making plans with Jason.

"Becker," she started, her voice pocked with nerves.

"Yes?" He opened his eyes.

"Did you mean it last night when you said maybe I should come back from time to time?"

He sat up straighter on the couch, looked her in the eyes. "Yes."

"Because I know we talked about just doing this" — she gestured from him to her — "while I'm in town. But I'm kind of thinking that maybe we can continue."

He nodded vigorously. "I want to keep seeing you." He said the words reverently, like a prayer. An offering.

Her heart pounded perilously close to her skin, as his lips curved into a small grin and his eyes sparkled. "Me, too."

"I can visit you, and you can come back here, and we can figure it out. My schedule is crazy, but there are plenty of days and nights when I'm off duty."

For a moment, Megan froze. *Off duty*. Those words were a sharp reminder of his job. For the last several hours she'd been enjoying their little corner of the world, all cozy and warm in his house, but this wasn't all there was. He could leave for duty at any moment and never come back. She knew that, had always known that, but she'd thought she'd swept that fear out the door.

The worry wasn't going away, though. It was creeping up on her now, a ghost leaving a cold imprint as it passed by.

"I'll be here, Megan. I'm not going anywhere," Becker said softly, as if he'd sensed the knot of fear that had set up camp. She tried to shoo it away by reminding herself that they were in limbo. But she still felt that nagging sense of unease. She'd hoped it would be gone by now, banished forever from her trunk of emotions. Yet there it was, taking some kind of hold anew. It didn't matter if she was leaving town. Didn't matter if their love affair ended now. She already cared too much. In seven days, in a month, in a year, whether she was in Portland or New York or Austin or someplace entirely new, she'd still care.

Was it easier to be the one with the dangerous job than the one who loved a man who took those risks? She didn't know, but her mind was racing into all sorts of debates and arguments that made her body feel cold.

"I think I'm going to jump in the shower," she said, hoping a few minutes alone under the hot stream of water would calm this new fleet of reckless nerves.

"Mind if I join you?"

"The brownies are going to be done in a few minutes. Can you get them out instead when the timer goes off?" she asked, because she needed to be alone.

"I can do that," he said and they pulled apart. As he turned into the kitchen, he tapped the on switch on a scanner. "Old habits die hard. Sometimes I just like to listen to what's going on."

As she stood under the hot water minutes later, she tried to talk herself down. Remind herself of how far she'd come. She scrubbed her skin, and washed her face, and let the stream of water pound onto her closed eyes. Soon, the tightness in her chest and in her heart started to fade.

As she turned off the water, she heard a loud, sharp sound.

Must have been the timer for the brownies, she figured.

She reached for a towel and dried off, but now there was movement. Footsteps. She heard Becker's voice. She couldn't make out the words, but he was talking on the phone. Rushed, but businesslike in tone. Her spine straightened.

Seconds later, there was a knock on the bathroom door,

then he opened it.

"I have to go. One of the old furniture warehouses down in Sandy Valley is on fire," he said.

"But Sandy Valley is thirty miles away. It's not even your—"

He cut her off. "It's moving fast. So they're asking for help. I'll call you later. I promise." He cupped her cheeks in his strong hands and pressed a gentle kiss against her forehead. "I promise," he said again.

He turned and left.

She knew how fire stations worked. Even if another station was called in for backup, only the men on duty went. Becker was *choosing* to go. He wasn't even on call, and he was making a choice to jump headfirst into danger.

As she heard the sound of the front door closing, she felt thrown back in time. A little girl again. Left. Scared. Alone. She hated that feeling. Hated it with a deep-seated passion that had been a part of her very makeup her entire life. She bit her lip, doing everything to fight the feeling. She towel-dried her hair. She pulled on her jeans. She grabbed her bra and shirt and shoved them on. Then her boots.

She didn't know when he'd be back, but she wasn't going to let the fear paralyze her. She'd simply finish the brownies, then head to her mom's house. Megan was looking forward to seeing her mom again.

There was a loud beeping sound that startled her. The brownies. She hustled into the kitchen, hunted for a pot-holder, and opened the oven door. She grabbed the baking pan and placed it on the counter, then considered the brownies from every angle.

Perfect. They looked perfect. She'd let them cool, then

cut them into squares, then arrange them on a plate, and leave Becker a nice, loving note. Maybe even draw a little raccoon for him, their mascot. He'd find it when he came home, and it would make him happy, knowing she'd done this for him while he was off fighting a blaze. He'd call her, and she'd finish up whatever she was doing, and she'd grab a change of clothes, come join him, and they'd spend the night together.

Everything would be fine.

She put that word on repeat in her head—*fine, fine, fine*—as she wandered around his house waiting for the brownies to cool. She needed to keep busy. She headed to the living room, surprised to find there were no framed photos on his mantel, not even of his brother. Then to his living room. There weren't any magazines on his table, or any books left out that he'd been in the middle of reading. Just his laptop and some printed spreadsheets that were probably from the Panting Dog. Her brief trip through his home revealed more proof that he was a loner with few signs of attachment. His love was his work, right? She returned to the kitchen, plopped down at the table, and thumbed aimlessly through the stack of newspapers.

She had nothing to hold on to.

Megan closed her eyes, squeezing them shut. Her mind skittered and raced. When had the fire in the warehouse started? How fast had it moved? How dangerous were the flames? She pictured beams falling, and sparks hissing, and men never coming back out. Her shoulders heaved and thick, salty tears fell. She swiped at her face. Stupid tears. Stupid fate.

Stupid her.

Because as much as her heart lurched for the men in the line of duty, her selfish soul ached, too.

This was some kind of reminder, wasn't it? This was the life of service, and a man in service was on call twenty-four hours a day. She knew that from her dad, and she knew that from Travis, and she might admire their work to the ends of the earth, but dammit. There was a reason she'd erected walls and set up boundaries.

Because she didn't want to know how it felt when the walls crumbled down.

This wasn't about a date interrupted. She could deal with that. What she was afraid of dealing with was the next time, and the next time, and then the time after that when he didn't come back, and might never come back.

She thought she'd made peace with the random zigs and zags of life. She'd even helped Becker realize that he didn't have to be beholden to the past. Hell, she believed all she'd said to him that night in the bar when her heart had finally cracked open, right along with his. But that was the problem with letting your heart open. It could hurt like hell.

And right now, it ached. So painfully. The prospect of losing him felt like a knife carving through her chest. She didn't just care for Becker; she'd fallen so far in such a short amount of time that she didn't know what she'd do without him. He was a part of her life, a part of her soul, a part of her future. She was terrified of never seeing him again because he meant the world to her now.

She returned to his bedroom, found her purse on the floor, and slung it on her shoulder. The covers on his bed were still messed up, and she latched onto a moment from last night, when he'd held her tight, and she'd felt warm and safe and oh so happy.

She clutched that image in her hands, grasping it. But she couldn't hold on. The memory slipped away.

She wheeled around, returned to the kitchen, dropped her purse on a chair, and tested the brownies. They were cool, so she sliced them and placed them on a plate, then washed the pan and the mixing bowls.

So domestic, the woman waiting for her man. Like her mom for so many years, waiting for a man who would never return.

Megan hated waiting. She needed to move, to swim, to travel.

She found a piece of paper and a pen in her purse. She started to write a note, to let him know she'd see him soon. But she only got as far as his name. She stared up at the ceiling, cycling through what to say next. As the shadows of the past gripped at her heart, she knew what to say. Because she didn't want to be the person who waited. If she stayed here, then she'd always be waiting with brownies for him.

With a trembling hand, she wrote a note.

Then she left, hopped on her bike, and rode, drowning out the noises in her head and the guilt in her heart as the wind dried her tears.

Chapter Twenty

Eleven hours later, Becker was dirty, wrung-out, and sore. The fire in the old furniture warehouse had been a vicious one, tearing across the building, all the tables and chairs becoming kindling that fed the flames. More than thirty men from stations all around the county had been called in to battle the blaze, and still it had taken more than half a day to put out the molten beast.

As dusk descended on Hidden Oaks, he pulled into his driveway, cut the engine, and rested his head against the back of the seat. He could barely move. The thought of opening the car door and walking up the front steps felt Herculean. But he'd promised himself that he'd call Megan as soon as he was inside, and the prospect of hearing her voice was all he needed to get his tired body out of the truck.

Just to listen to her for a minute, as he collapsed on the couch and drifted off into sleep, was a balm to his soul, so he held on to that thought as he trudged up to his front door, unlocked it wearily, and yawned once he stepped inside. A yawn that seemed to last for years and threatened to slam his eyelids down. But somehow he made it up his steps as he fumbled through his contacts on his phone, looking for her number. He found it as he walked into the kitchen. He hit dial and waited. Then he noticed a plate of brownies as it rang. And rang. And rang.

There was a note folded in two on top of the brownies. A sense of peace rippled through his bones. She'd left him a note that first night, and she'd kept doing it. It was her thing, and he loved that he was part of something deeply meaningful to her. Her art; the way she expressed herself. He opened it, expecting to see a crazy drawing of a llama wearing a suit and a few clever little lines about seeing him again soon. But instead, he found only words. They looked terribly naked against the white paper without her pictures.

Hi Becker,

You're off doing your job right now and my head is a mess, and my heart is shredding. My hands are shaking as I write this. But all I can think about now is losing you. It's all I see, and all I can picture, and this hurts so much. I know what I'm feeling right now doesn't compare to how you must have felt when you lost your friends. Maybe that's why I need to go. Because I DO know what it might feel like if you don't come back. I DO know what it looks like. I lived it for years. The more time I spend with you, the harder I fall. And the worse it will hurt. Because I'm already in love with you.

Megan.

His heart buzzed momentarily with happiness, as he read and reread the last sentence, both beautiful and painful. But the joy was far too short-lived. Because what did it matter if she was in love with him if she wouldn't let herself be with him? He rubbed a soot-covered hand over his jaw and shook his head. He wished the heaviness he felt inside was just from work. That the sadness was from something else. But it was from her. From the way he cruelly learned how a new kind of missing felt.

He should have known better. She didn't settle. She didn't stay. She picked up and left; she'd done it since she was a kid. Moving through life from town to town, from secret hideout to secret hideout, was her way of dealing with life's challenges. He should have been prepared for this. He'd always known she was bending to the point of breaking with him. But as he made his way to the closest horizontal surface, knowing all that didn't stop his chest from hurting and his heart from aching.

He collapsed onto the couch, too tired to move, too worn out to do anything but ball up the note and toss it down the stairs. He could run and find her today. Or tomorrow. Or the next day. Try to convince her. Prove to her they were worth it. That falling for him wouldn't be the scariest thing she'd ever do. But that would be a lie. Because being with him _was_ scary to her, and he wanted to respect where she drew the line, even though it hurt like hell.

It hurt worse than his body felt right now.

That's why he pushed himself up from the couch, flashing to the night in his bar when she helped him start to let go of the fear that had clutched at him. He didn't know that she needed help right now, but he knew one thing about himself that was steady and constant—no matter the outcome, he had to try his hardest.

She might have left him, but she'd also told him something he couldn't ignore.

He stood up and grabbed his keys. He knew where she was.

• • •

She swiped away a final tear. She refused to cry anymore. She'd cried enough on the hours she spent riding around on her bike before she returned to the river. She didn't deserve to shed tears. Sucking in a deep breath to quiet her aching heart, she tried desperately to pull herself together as the water slipped over rocks. The river didn't care that she'd come here through the years—to escape, to play, to be alone. The river didn't need her, but it was always here. It never left; it never went away. It was steady and reliable as it traveled downstream, along the bends and curves in the riverbed, cut over the years by time. The one constant in her life—the one sure thing.

She drew her knees up to her chest, tucking herself in tight against the cold stone of the rock behind her. She stared at the scene before her, the trees curling their branches over the river, the rocks and paths carved through the woods that hugged the water. In the distance, she spotted a squirrel racing along a low branch, perhaps in hot pursuit of an acorn. She pictured him comically drawn, running on two sturdy little legs, arms outstretched and reaching. She'd surely never ink a squirrel tattoo for someone, but she liked to see the real world in caricature sometimes. That had always helped her to deal, to handle the vacancies she'd felt when she was younger—first her dad, then her mom. They had both been gone in different ways.

Though she came here alone today after hours and hours on her bike, no pens or sketch pad with her, she outlined the squirrel's image in her mind, shading in his chest, drawing an oversize tail. The image brought a small smile to her lips. Becker would have liked it. She would have liked giving it to him.

She cringed. Hearing his name in her head brought a fresh wave of shame through her. She was a coward. She'd run because she couldn't deal.

She wanted to ask the river all the questions in her heart. She wanted to know the answers to the fears that gnawed away at her. But there would never be any answers. There was only one person who had the answers for her. As the sun began to fall in the sky, she headed in that direction.

• • •

She hadn't been at the river. Her bike hadn't been in the parking lot at the foot of the trail, but he'd still scoured all the secret spots she'd shown him by the rocks, and the water, and along the path. The light was fading as the sun crept behind the hills. He'd known, deep in his gut, that she wasn't there. But he'd had to check because he'd been so sure he'd find her.

A cruel possibility swooped down as he walked away from the river. Had she left already for Portland? Megan had it in her, but would she really just leave? Then again, she'd told him about leaving her ex and that had been a swift exit. Was this how she ended things? With a good-bye note, and then she tore out of town? She might already be in Oregon by now, settling in somewhere downtown, finding new friends to connect with, a new place to call her own, until she threw her sparse belongings together once more and moved on to the next town, the itinerant artist, picking up whenever she was ready for a new adventure.

As darkness inched closer, the shadows playing against the woods, he returned to his truck and drove back to town. He tried Jamie's house, but she hadn't heard from Megan and promised she'd let him know when she did. He checked out Travis's place, but there were no signs of her there, either. Maybe he should have gone to her mom's first, but it was his last hope, so he saved it for last. This was the closest thing she had to a home, and even though Megan had wanderlust, she also loved her home.

When he turned onto her mom's street, he was greeted with a beautiful sight. Her bike in the driveway. He pulled up and turned off his truck. He was about to head straight to the door and knock when he stopped himself. What was he going to say? How was he going to convince her to take a chance on him?

Sitting in the quiet of his truck, he flicked on the light and reread her note, still wrinkled from when he'd balled it up. What was his grand plan to convince her she could give up all her fears for him? He knew himself well enough to know that he wasn't going to quit the firehouse. Sure, he'd toyed with the idea and had let his imagination run wild with the possibility of just being a bar owner. But his other job mattered too much to him; it was part of who he was, come hell or high water. It was written in his blood, and imprinted on his heart since he was a kid. Megan had understood deeply when he told her that story. He was a firefighter no matter what, and if he wasn't willing or able to let go of that, how the hell was he going to convince her to stay with him?

Her note was clear. She couldn't be with him.

But he had something to tell her. She'd always left him notes, some sweet, some sexy, some sad. He needed to do the same. He rooted around in his glove compartment for a piece of paper and a pen, and then scratched out a few quick lines. Then he folded it over, wrote her name on the front, and tucked it safely alongside the oil gauge on her bike.

• • •

The sound of the dryer rattling in the nearby mudroom was oddly comforting to Megan as she crossed and uncrossed her legs, waiting for the tea to steep. She'd already helped her mom unpack, started a load of laundry from the trip, and now moved it over to the dryer. Robert was back at work already at An Open Book, and her mom had brewed a pot of tea. Her mom poured the tea, brought the mugs to the table, and handed one to Megan.

"Tell me everything. Was the cruise amazing?" Megan asked as she wrapped her hands around the warm ceramic.

Her mom tilted her head and gave her a quizzical look. "Sweetie, you've already asked me that about ten times."

"Oh. Yeah, I did," she admitted. She'd thought this would be easy. But it wasn't the least bit simple to get the words out, so she'd distracted herself.

"What's wrong? You don't seem like yourself. Is it Jason still? Is that whole thing ending getting you down?"

Megan managed a bitter laugh. "I wish. I wish it were Jason."

Her mom narrowed her eyebrows in question. "What is it that's getting you down?"

Megan sighed heavily and slumped in her chair. She pushed a hand through her hair. She'd ridden clear up to Tahoe and back, and the cool air on her face and the wind at her back had done nothing to clear her head or her heart of that man. She ached for Becker, and she hated feeling this way. She wanted him out of her system, far away. But running had done nothing to abate her desire for him.

"You know our hall, Mom? With all the pictures?"

She nodded.

"And how it almost seems as if there are a few years missing?"

Her mom smiled sadly. "I know, sweetie. I was a mess there for some time."

"You were. It's like you were gone," she said, keeping her voice steady and strong. They'd talked about her mom's depression before; they'd come to peace with it. But there was more that needed to be said.

"I was gone. If I could do anything over in my life, that would be it. I was a shell of a person for a few years there, and they were vital years for you. I know I failed you then," she said, reaching her hand across the table to grasp Megan's. She squeezed back. She wasn't mad at her mom. The time for anger had passed long ago. "I'm glad you had Travis, though. You two were amazing kids, and you really took care of yourselves during a time when I wasn't capable of it."

"I wish you were there for us. I do. And there's nothing that scares me more in the whole world than becoming like that."

Her mom quirked up an eyebrow in question.

"I love you, but I don't want to be like you," Megan said and took a sip of her tea. The simple physical act of drinking the hot beverage kept her steady as they talked.

"Why would you be like me? You're strong, and you've made it pretty much clear to the entire world that you're not going to make the same mistake."

The word pierced her. *Mistake.* Was Becker a mistake? If he was, she could let him go. She could be on her bike right now, riding to Portland, finishing up the final details of the calendar from the next state. But she hadn't managed to cross the California border yet. The wings on her feet weren't working as well as they used to. They were heavier, keeping her rooted *here.*

The weight of the admission was heavy on her shoulders as she whispered, "I already have."

Her mom squeezed her hand harder, her eyes full of warmth. "Am I to understand that means you've fallen for a firefighter?"

Megan had never been one to lie to her mom or to hold things back from her. When her mom had come out on the other side of depression, Megan had been right there, ready for her. She told her nearly everything about Becker. She spilled the details of her heart, how he made her feel, how he understood her hopes and dreams, how he encouraged her, how he made her laugh, and most of all, how very much he cared. Her mom scooted her chair closer and wrapped a comforting arm around her daughter's shoulders. "He sounds pretty fantastic," she said.

"He is," Megan croaked out. "That's the problem."

Her mom nodded sympathetically. "I know. Believe me,

I know. Your father was magic to me and I loved him with every ounce of my heart and soul. It's not easy loving a man like that, is it?"

A lone tear streaked down Megan's cheek. She batted the mutinous thing away and shook her head in answer.

"But as heartbroken as I was, as devastated as I was, I wouldn't have traded a day with your father. You need to know that, sweetie." Her mom placed a gentle hand on her chin and made Megan look at her. "I know I wasn't there for you. I know I checked out, I know I wasn't around when you needed me to be, and I'm so very sorry. But if it weren't for your dad, I wouldn't have you and Travis, and you guys are the best things that ever happened to me. Life can't be scripted and it can hardly even be planned. And you can't control who you fall for. Sometimes, you just have to take the risk."

Her mother's words were soft and tender, yet they cut her more sharply than a knife, more deeply than all those lonely nights without Jason when he'd been off loving something more than her. But here was a man who was so much more than Jason. Who'd run into a building to fight a fire.

She let her choices unfold in front of her. Should she take the risk or let him pass her by? She'd felt so certain when she fled from his house, but now after talking to her mom, she wanted to find a way to be okay with the risk, with the choice she longed to make. She desperately wanted to choose him over fear, but she'd spent so much of her life packing ice around her heart so she could avoid pain.

"You think I should take this risk, then?"

"That's entirely up to you. But all I will tell you is this," her mom added. "Do I wish I had more time with your father? Yes. Do I regret the time we had? Never. Not a moment of it. He was worth it."

Funny, how after all her walls, all her rules, all her rigid guidelines about not getting involved with a fireman, it turned out what she needed most was a man like Becker. The fact that she'd been the only one to say "I'm in love with you" barely crossed her mind. She knew he felt the same. She was as certain of his feelings as she was of her own.

How stupid had she been to run? How foolish did she have to be to leave him a note saying "I love you, but goodbye"? She was going to prove that she was worthy of him too. She couldn't just show up on his doorstep and say she was sorry. No, she was going to show him that she was done running, and that she was hooked.

She wasn't sure how, but she was going to figure it out.

There was a knock on the door. For a brief moment, her heart beat in double time, thinking it was Becker. But then the knock played in the rhythm of "Shave and a Haircut." It was Travis.

"I invited him for dinner," her mom said.

"I'll let him in," Megan said, as she left the kitchen and headed to the front door.

Travis stood in the doorway, brandishing a note. "I saw this on your bike. And I think I know who it's from."

Chapter Twenty-One

With shaky fingers, she began unfolding the paper. She didn't have to recognize the handwriting on the front to know who it was from. She *knew*. Her heart lodged itself in her throat as she opened the note.

Megan,

I thought you'd be gone by now. But you're still here, and I want to believe that's good. Only you can tell me where we go from here. Because here's the thing—I'm in love with you too.

Becker

She looked up at her brother and her mom. Her hands were trembling, and she was sure they could read her every emotion that was ping-ponging through her body as fear turned to hope.

"Well?" her mom asked.

"It seems I'm in love with someone who's in love with me too."

She waited for Travis to curse or cringe, to tell her she was foolish. But he didn't. Instead, he wrapped an arm around her and squeezed her shoulder. "What are we going to do about that, Megan?"

Surprise took over her features. "You never call me Megan."

"I know. But I need to start, since that's what you prefer. And if you two fools are in love, far be it from me to stop it. Let's figure this shit out."

"Travis," their mom chided. "Watch your mouth."

"Sorry, Mom."

"Now, come inside, sit down, have some dinner, and let's come up with a plan."

"Yes, Mom," she and Travis said in unison, and there was something darn near perfect about this moment—the roles in her family were as they should be. Her brother was her brother, her mother was her mother, and she was her own woman. They were going to help her figure out what to do next. They'd been fractured years before, but now they were a family working together.

. . .

He tried to pretend he wasn't counting the hours since he'd left that note. But he was no good at that kind of lie. It had been thirteen hours and twenty-two minutes with no word from her. Granted, he'd managed a dreamless sleep for most of that time, and his body had needed it after fighting that fire wrung him dry. Ironic, that he always slept the best when he'd been battling a massive fire. Now, he and Smith were finishing up a talk at the local elementary school on fire safety.

"What are the three words you're going to remember after today?" Smith asked the group of first graders, and Becker had to hand it to the guy. He could work a room like nobody's business. He had the local six-year-olds eating out of the palms of his hands. Enrapt.

"Stop, drop, and roll," the kids shouted in unison, and Smith gave them a rousing applause. "Now, who wants to see a fire truck?"

His friend led the group from the small classroom and to the truck stationed outside the elementary school. The kids happily scampered around the engine, with Becker and Smith showing them how everything worked, even plunking down plastic helmets on their heads if they wanted to pretend they were firemen too. Most of the boys did. That was normal; this was a job that a lot of kids *said* they wanted to grow up and do. But for the first time, there was a low voice in Becker's head that wanted him to warn the kids to find another job.

Okay, so no one was signing up for duty at the ripe old age of six, but he almost wanted to tell them there's a flip side to the job. That it can mean you're man against the world. That it can mean you can't have other things. Can't want them. Shouldn't want them.

"Fuck," he muttered as he pushed a hand through his dark hair as soon as the demonstration was over, and the first graders had started to march back into their school. But a lone straggler overheard him and looked up.

Ah, hell.

"You okay, sir?" the little kid asked. The girl had sweet,

wide eyes and rosy cheeks.

"Just fine. Just thinking about something. Why don't you let me walk you back inside?"

The girl nodded, and then started chattering about the end of the school year, and how she was going to teach her family stop, drop, and roll. "I think everyone needs to know that. I'm glad you were here today, sir, as a community helper," she said, repeating the words the teacher had used to introduce them.

"And I am glad to be here, too," he said, smiling as he held open the door. The girl ran the rest of the way into the school, and Becker returned to the truck where Smith was waiting.

"Better watch your language in front of the kiddies," Smith teased.

"Yeah, or they'll figure out I'm an asshole, right?" he said.

Smith gave him a steady stare, turning serious. "What's your deal, Beck? Never seen you so wound up before at one of these things. You usually keep your shit together. The warehouse get to you?"

"It's nothing," he muttered, staring out the window as Smith turned the key in the ignition. It had to be nothing. He'd opened his heart to her, and she hadn't responded. She'd meant it then when she said being with him hurt too much. He'd hoped and wished that telling her how he felt, that laying his feelings on the line, would have sent her running back to his arms. But the issue had never been how they felt. The issue was whether she'd *let* herself feel for him. Her silence was her answer. She wouldn't. Because of who he was.

"All righty. Well, that's a whole lot of nothing that's

turning you into a whole lot of pissed off," Smith said as they pulled away from the school to head back to the firehouse. He looked at Becker and screwed up his face in a pissy, annoyed imitation of what Becker must have looked like. "You're all worked up about something, aren't you?"

He scrubbed a hand over his jaw and shook his head. Not what he wanted to get into right now. He had to start pushing the thoughts of her far away, tucking them into that trunk in the back of his mind.

"Let me guess. I'm gonna use my crazy powers of deduction. But I'm willing to bet that my little lady's best chickadee is the one who's got you out of sorts."

Becker turned to Smith and narrowed his eyes. "What?"

Smith nodded knowingly. "Ah, so I'm right?"

"I have no idea what you're talking about."

"Aww, that's cute."

"What's cute?" Becker muttered.

"That you think that shit will work with me. Let me refresh your memory. Remember the night of the Spring Festival when I was all out of sorts about Jamie and I asked for your advice? You saw right through me, and you knew I was talking about her."

"Yes," Becker admitted grudgingly, remembering how he of all people had urged Smith to be direct with Jamie about how he felt.

"Besides, I've seen the two of you together, and you've got it bad for each other. So what's the problem?"

Becker heaved a sigh. Smith was relentless, but the truth was he was wound tight again, and he might as well stop keeping every single painful thought and feeling to himself. He'd done that for the last year and he hadn't started to feel human again until he finally talked about it with Megan. "The problem is many problems. I'm crazy about her and want her back, but she's leaving town," he said, starting with the list of roadblocks. "And she's afraid of being with me—"

Smith cut him off before he could voice Megan's deeper fears.

"Ah, now we're getting somewhere," Smith said as he turned onto the street with the firehouse, ready and eager to dispense advice, it seemed. "All right, here's my best channeling of Dr. Phil advice. Go with her."

He scrunched his eyebrows. "Go with her?"

Smith nodded vigorously as he pulled into the station. "Yep. If you love her, if you're crazy for her, and the only thing standing in the way is her leaving town, then go with her."

It wasn't that simple, he wanted to say.

But then, maybe it was.

Because thirty minutes later, Travis strolled into the firehouse and clapped him on the shoulder. "Hey man, we need to talk."

"Yeah?" He raised an eyebrow, curiosity digging deep into him. The last time they'd talked here at the firehouse, Travis had made it patently clear that their friendship was history if he hurt Megan. He'd done just that, hadn't he? Becker braced himself for the final nail in the coffin.

"Yeah, because I'm about to take over the rest of your shift. My sister is waiting for you at your house, and I really think you need to go see her right now. Because you're the best man in the world for her, and there's nothing I want more than for her to be happy."

Becker didn't move. He was sure his boots were stuck

to the concrete floor, and that his ears were playing tricks on him. Because there was no way Travis had said that. No fucking way. "You didn't just say what I think you said, did you?"

Travis rolled his eyes. "Get the hell out of here."

"No, seriously, Trav," he said, pushing back. He needed to know for certain. "She's still here?"

"Yes. I offered to bring her here to the firehouse to see you and talk to you, like in some goddamn chick movie where one of them shows up at the other's workplace to profess their feelings in front of the world, but she said something about the two of you being *anti-crowd*. So there you go. She's still here, at your house, and you have my blessing. Not that you ever needed it," Travis grumbled. "Nor did she, because she's a grown woman and not just my baby sister, and she's chosen you. If you make her this goddamn happy that she's chucked the biggest worry she ever had, then far be it from little old me to stand in the way."

Becker laughed, maybe from the shock, maybe from the sheer volume of this double whammy of a surprise. "No. I didn't need it, and she didn't, either. But I'm damn glad to have it, bro."

Travis clapped Becker on the back, and then moved it for a quick hug. "Now go," Travis said, shooing him away. "I don't come around often and take other men's shifts for grins. *Go*."

Chapter Twenty-Two

She'd replayed those two little words from her mom—*worth it*—on the way down to San Francisco this morning with Travis, then in the hour she'd sat in the chair, gritting her teeth because it hurt, and all the way back to Hidden Oaks, straight into Becker's driveway. Travis had kept her company this time, a marked contrast to the last time she'd been in that shop in the city.

Now she was waiting on his doorstep, the noontime sun shining brightly above. This time, she didn't mind waiting for him under the blue sky of a summer day. She wouldn't mind waiting in the rain, or the wind, or the dark of the night either. He was worth waiting for, even as the nerves skated across her skin, and the hummingbirds raced in circles in her belly. She didn't know if he would take her back. She didn't know if she'd lost her chance. But she knew she had to take the risk.

When he pulled up several minutes after Travis had left

for the fire station, she practically wanted to run to his truck, yank open the door, and fling herself at him. Instead, she rose as he stepped out of his vehicle. Then they both stopped moving. There was a moment when they simply stood in place, she on the steps, he in the driveway, staring at each other. This was the moment—the real start or end to them.

She took the first step and began walking across his lawn, and in seconds he was walking toward her.

"Hi," she said as she neared him. She kept her hands at her sides, even though she wanted to throw her arms around him and kiss him. But words needed to come first. She would assume nothing, even though he was here.

"Hi."

She swallowed and started to talk, to say she was sorry, to say she loved him, to say all the things she'd realized in the last twenty-four hours, but he went first. "Megan, I'll go with you to Portland."

She blinked. That was the last thing in the world she'd thought she would hear. He loved Hidden Oaks. It had become the place where he belonged. "What? But you love it here."

"I do. I never thought I'd get so attached to a town, especially when I was trying to escape everything, but this town has become my family—from the people I work with at the bar, to the woman who makes my coffee, to all the men at the firehouse. I came here to start over and somehow over the last year it worked; they've all snuck in on me and I'll miss them like hell," he said, stopping to reach for her and run his fingers through her hair.

She leaned into his hand, wanting to be close to him.

"But you," he continued, looking at her with such reverence. "You gave me a purpose. You gave me myself back.

I'm in love with you. Truly and deeply in love with you, and I never expected it to happen, but then I never expected *you* to happen. I never expected you to walk—or *crash* really—into my life and change nearly everything about what I want. And even though I can never give up the firehouse, I can give up this town that has become a home. I can give up my bar. I can give up my friends, but I can't give up you," he said, and her throat hitched, her eyes welling with tears. She reached for his hand, threading her fingers through his. She squeezed his hand, her way of telling him to keep going because he seemed to have more to say, and she wanted to hear it all. Every beautiful word.

"You are what's most important to me, and I want you to have all the things you want in life, including your art and the tattoo shop that I know you're going to have there someday, and your hopes and your dreams. And I hope and I dream that I can be a part of all that if you'll have me, and I know that's asking a lot. I can't promise you that I won't get hurt, but I can promise you I will do everything I can to come home to you. Wherever we are."

We.

Her mind spun wildly as he put himself on the line for her and offered her something she'd never expected. Her heart rioted in her chest, dancing like a madwoman. She couldn't hold back. She reached for him, looping a hand around his neck, lacing her fingers through his soft hair. Instantly, she felt him relax under her touch.

"I want nothing more than to have you with me," she said, her voice breaking as stupid tears of joy threatened to overwhelm her.

"You do?" he asked carefully.

"I do," she said quickly. "Yes, I do. So much. And I'm sorry I ran. I'm sorry I freaked out. I was scared because I feel so much for you that I don't know what to do with it. It's more than I ever thought I would feel." She held out her hands, as if she were surrendering. Maybe she was—surrendering to love. "This is a done deal. This thing I feel for you isn't going to go away. Nothing is going to undo it."

"Are you sure?" he asked with concern in his eyes, but he moved closer to her, running his hand along her hip, then around her waist. She loved the feel of his hand on her. She didn't want to let go of him.

"Yes," she said, fighting back the tears, even though they were good tears this time. They were tears that came from a heart that was cracking wide open, not one she was trying to protect. "I was scared, and I'm still scared, but I want to be scared with you, here or in Portland or wherever we are. My heart belongs to you, and that's not going to change whether I stay by your side or run. Loving you plays on every fear I've had since I was young. But I'm a grown-up now, and even though it took me a day to come to my stupid senses, I've come to them. Because I've fallen for you, and not just the bar owner I met the first night, but the guy who fights his way in and out of burning buildings. That's who you are and that's the man I'm in love with."

• • •

They'd both used the L-word in their letters to each other. But today, they were saying it in person. He was hearing it fall on his ears as she looked at him with tenderness and trust. He flashed back to the night they met, to how simple it had seemed then. Now it was simple, but only because when you look in the eyes of the woman who changes your heart, everything is simple.

Amazingly, beautifully simple and true in its own way. Not every woman was going to sign up for the roller coaster of loving a man like him. But she wasn't just any woman. She was his.

He cupped her cheek in his hand, and she leaned into him instantly. He gently ran the back of his fingers across her soft skin. "I'm so in love with you," he said, then brushed his lips against hers because he couldn't wait any longer to kiss her.

Kissing her was like coming home. The feel of her lips was passion and certainty all at once. It was everything he'd never known he wanted, and everything he could never give up. He slanted his mouth to hers, and didn't stop kissing her. His pulse raced, vibrations soaring through his body. Her lips tasted spectacular, and even though it had been only a day since she'd seen him, it felt like forever. She kissed him back as if it had been, as if she'd been waiting for his return.

Finally, they pulled apart.

"Should we get packing?" he said with a smile. He was ready. He'd go anywhere with her. "I've got a truck; I can give my two weeks and we can get out of town."

Her brown eyes glinted playfully. "I've got that all fig-ured out, and I'll tell you everything in a minute. But there's something I want to show you first."

She started stripping again. Just like when he'd met her. She winced as she unbuttoned her shirt and pulled it off. She wore only a white tank top underneath. She turned slightly to show him her bare shoulder, which was no longer bare. It was marked up with new ink.

His lips quirked up at the sight of her new tattoo to match the owl. The raccoon she'd drawn was now permanent on her skin.

"You have a raccoon firefighter on your shoulder," he said in disbelief.

"Do you like it?" she asked, her voice wavering.

"I love it." He gazed at the drawing she'd made that was now a part of her body. He looked in her eyes. They were soft and sweet and full of everything he'd ever wanted. "Just like I love you."

"It's permanent," she said, gesturing to her new ink. "Like how I feel for you." Then she wrapped herself up in him, pressing herself against his chest, and the feel of her perfect body was both too much and never enough. He needed her now.

"Good. Now let's get inside so I can have you again and then you can tell me your plans."

. . .

Her hands were on his waist, pulling up his navy-blue T-shirt as he shut the door behind them. She couldn't keep her hands off him. She was dying to share her plan, but she wanted him now. Talking would need to be tabled. Contact came first. "Let's do it on the stairs," she said. "I can't wait."

"Trust me, I plan on fucking you on my stairs, and in my shower, and on the couch, and bent over the counter, but right now I am taking you back to my bedroom, and I am making love to you, and you're not going to want to leave again."

He picked her up, sensitive to her tender tattooed flesh, and slung her over his shoulder. He took the stairs two at a time. It was a possessive move, and a protective one, and it said everything she'd ever need to know about him. He was fierce, and he was gentle, and he was all she wanted. He carried her back to his bed and laid her down.

"And now, where did we leave off?" He tapped his index finger against his chin as if he were deep in thought, then smiled wickedly. She loved that he smiled so much with her. That he'd gone from brooding to a little less brooding.

She knew she hadn't turned him into a new man. He was still Becker. He still had that loner side and probably always would. But at least he'd started to move beyond what had chased him here in the first place. "Ah, I seem to remember. I'd turned you into a rag doll, but you were starting to get ready for another round."

"I'm ready." She skimmed off her jeans and reached for his belt buckle, pulling him close. She angled her hips into him, her body a magnet needing its opposite. He dipped his hand into her panties, groaning when he felt her dampness.

"You're so wet for me," he said, his voice low and husky, his tone revealing how much he savored everything they had together. The connection, the desire, the love.

"I love the way you touch me. I love everything about it," she said, her breathing already turning shallow as he stroked her.

"The feeling is so completely mutual." He took her hand, showing her how aroused he was, pressing her palm against his erection, straining the denim of his jeans. He was so thick and hard, and she desperately needed to feel him. She un-zipped his pants, slid them down his hips, and took his hard length in her hand. "Seems we're a good fit," she murmured. "Now, think you've got a condom you could put on right about now? Because I can't wait anymore for you."

He stepped out of his jeans all the way, removed his shirt, and rolled on a condom. He settled between her legs and sank into her. He stilled for a moment, took a deep breath, as if being inside her was sending him to another realm too.

Then he made love to her, soft and tender, stroking inside her, whispering to her all the things he loved about her, as she whimpered and gasped and thanked the world that they'd both come to their senses, because there was nothing better than this, than him, than them.

"Come with me now, Becker," she whispered.

She wrapped her legs as tightly around him as she could, gripping his hips in her thighs, holding him deep as he groaned and she cried out, and they came together.

Then, as he held her close in his arms, she turned down his offer to move with her.

• • •

He tensed all over. "You don't want me to go with you?"

Hell, he'd been crazy to suggest packing up everything and leaving town. That was kind of presumptuous, wasn't it?

"No," she said with a wild grin, like she had a fantastic secret.

"Then what?"

"I'm staying in town."

His eyes widened in shock. "You are? But what about Portland? What about the tattoo shop and the job?"

"I'll visit Portland. Besides, the reason I dreamed of

going was that I didn't have a place I wanted to stay. I was trying on new towns. Now I do have a place where I want to be. I want to stay here. Hidden Oaks is my home. My mom is here, Travis is here, the bookstore is here, Jamie's here, my favorite coffee shop is here, and the river is here..." she said, letting her voice trail off in a tease.

"And? Anything else here that belongs on that list of your favorite things?"

"And you're here," she added, snuggling closer to him. "So I'm staying."

"I'm officially the happiest man in the world now," he said, and all the tension left his body. "But what are you going to do? I want you to be happy."

"Don't worry. I have a plan."

Epilogue

She'd used many canvasses in the last few months, but Becker's shoulder was by far her favorite. As she finished the final letter of his ink, she smiled to herself, pleased with her work. He'd been rock-solid in the chair, not flinching and barely tensing as she marked his skin. She hadn't minded either that he'd been shirtless, though of course she'd seen him clothes-free countless times. Still, the look and feel of his beautiful body had not grown old. In fact, the more she had him, the more of him she wanted.

Fortunately, they lived together now, so she was able to have him as much as she wanted. She'd bounced around town for a bit, crashing at her mom's some nights, at other times staying at Jamie's when Jamie was with Smith. But that had only lasted so long. Becker had wanted her in his home, and that's where she wanted to be, too.

"All right. That's a wrap," she said, setting down her tools and spinning him a few inches so he could see his first tattoo in the mirror.

He angled his shoulder slightly to get a better look, and she watched as he took it in. She loved this moment—when clients first saw their tattoos. It was a priceless reaction, and his meant so much to her. Because it was him, and because of what he'd chosen—the initials of his two fallen friends from Chicago.

He'd moved past the pain that had hobbled him, and now he'd found strength in the memories of those friendships. This was another way to remember them, he'd said when he told her he wanted her to ink him. It had been his idea completely and she was thrilled that he'd come to it on his own, and delighted that she'd get to do it.

"It's perfect," he said softly, with reverence in his voice. She bent over and kissed his hair. "Thank you," he added.

"No, thank you for choosing my shop for your first tattoo," she said, then gestured to the tiny little place she owned and operated in Hidden Oaks. Her mom had been about to expand the café at her bookstore, but since their town was bereft of a tattoo shop, she'd given the additional space to Megan.

"Mom, I can't take it. This is your store. Your space," Megan had said when her mom made the offer.

"Please. It's my gift to you. It's the least I can do."

Megan relented, understanding deeply why her mom wanted to do it. "Then I accept this amazing gift."

Smith had quickly shifted gears with the construction, turning the unfinished space into a tattoo shop, while Megan moonlighted at her friend's tattoo parlor in San Francisco.

She finished her apprenticeship there, until both she and the shop in her hometown were ready. She created the sign that hung on the window that looked out on the town square. PAINT MY BODY. Every town needed a tattoo shop; this was the first one in Hidden Oaks.

"As if I'd choose anyplace else but the shop you named for me," Becker said, leaning back in the chair and reaching for her, roping his arms around her.

She pointed to the calendar that hung on the wall, open to his month—November—and the shot of him by the river after they'd painted each other. "My inspiration for the name looks at me every day as I work."

"Speaking of work, I need to get going. My shift starts soon," he said as he stood and pulled on his shirt.

"I'll see you tomorrow when it's over."

"Yes. You will."

He gave her a soft and sweet kiss, the kind that said he'd be coming home to her. As she kissed him back, she was telling him without words that she had all the faith in the world that he'd be walking through the door tomorrow.

Acknowledgments

Thank you to all my amazing readers, who blow my mind every day with their passion for reading. Thank you to my editors, Stacy and Alycia, who helped me find the true love between Megan and Becker. Thank you to my agent Michelle for her guiding insight.

The fantastically talented Samanthe Beck read an early draft and provided invaluable insight. I am indebted to my eagle-eye readers Tanya Farrell and Kim Bias for making sure the story was all it could be. My author buddies are my writing family and I adore Jessie Evans, Monica Murphy, Sawyer Bennett, Melody Grace, Violet Duke, Lexi Ryan, and Kendall Ryan.

To all the brave men and women who put their lives on the line every day in the fire service — I am ever grateful for your courage.

Most of all, thank you to my family for making every day worthwhile.

And of course, thanks to my pets for being awesome. Dogs rule.

About the Author

Lauren Blakely writes sexy contemporary romance novels with heat, heart, and humor, and many of her books have appeared on the *New York Times*, USA TODAY, Amazon, Barnes and Noble, and iBooks bestseller lists. Like the heroine in her novel, *Far Too Tempting*, she thinks life should be filled with family, laughter, and the kind of love that love songs promise. Lauren lives in California with her husband, children, and dogs. She also writes for young adults under the name Daisy Whitney.

www.laurenblakely.com

Discover Lauren Blakely's **Fighting Fire** *series...*

BURN FOR ME

Jamie Lansing has had it bad for firefighter Smith Grayson for as long as they've been friends. Yes, he's ridiculously charming and she might stare a little too long at his abs, but his dirty-talking, rough-around-the-edges ways aren't for her. But Smith has only ever had eyes for Jamie. When she suggests a week of no-strings-attached sex to get him out of her system, Smith knows this is his one chance to prove he's not just the man she needs in her bed, but the man she needs in her life.

Also by Lauren Blakely

FAR TOO TEMPTING

CAUGHT UP IN HER

CAUGHT UP IN US

PRETENDING HE'S MINE

PLAYING WITH HER HEART

TROPHY HUSBAND

STARS IN THEIR EYES

FAR TOO TEMPTING

THE THRILL OF IT

THE START OF US

EVERY SECOND WITH YOU

NIGHT AFTER NIGHT

AFTER THIS NIGHT

ONE MORE NIGHT

CPSIA information can be obtained
at www.ICGtesting.com
Printed in the USA
BVOW03s1826121017
497525BV00001B/6/P

9 781511 705448